I REACHED FOR THE HANDLE OF MY GUN AND GRIPPED IT.

"Start your play," said Waters, or rather, the evil spirit that was in Waters then.

But just at that, with a split part of a second to go, Chip pushed in between us.

"Leave this off!" said he.

"Get out of my way!" said Waters, and with a back hand cuff, he knocked the boy sprawling.

Then he saw, in a flash, and I saw, too.

There wasn't enough force in that blow to have floored the real Chip, made of rawhide and whalebone as he was. But the boy had gone down, and staring in wonder at him as he lay on his back, I saw a red-stained bandage around his right leg, above the knee; and Waters saw it, too, and groaned as though a bullet had torn through his own flesh. . . .

Books by Max Brand

Published by POCKET BOOKS

Max Brand
TROUBLE KID

PUBLISHED BY POCKET BOOKS NEW YORK

POCKET BOOKS, a Simon & Schuster division of
GULF & WESTERN CORPORATION
1230 Avenue of the Americas, New York, N.Y. 10020

Copyright 1931 by Street and Smith Publications, Inc.;
copyright renewed © 1959 by Dorothy Faust

Published by arrangement with Dodd, Mead & Company

All rights reserved, including the right to reproduce
this book or portions thereof in any form whatsoever.
For information address Dodd, Mead & Company,
79 Madison Avenue, New York, N.Y. 10016

ISBN: 0-671-83028-7

First Pocket Books printing February, 1972

10   9   8   7   6   5   4

Trademarks registered in the United States and other countries.

Printed in the U.S.A.

TROUBLE KID

PART ONE

Chapter One

If he had had a quarter of an inch of rain a year, Newbold could have raised cattle in Hades. For that matter, we all felt that his range was a little worse than Hades; it averaged only a shade more than a quarter of an inch of rain most of the year.

What saved him, of course, was the western half of the range, where the westerlies piled up clouds at certain times of the year and gave that smaller section of his land a good drenching. When the grass petered out all to the east and south, we had to get the cows started through the teeth of the passes and work them over to the green section. They were a hump-backed lot, all gaunted up with thirst and the grass famine, before we got them to the western range, however. And after they hit the green feed they went at it so hard that a lot of them were sick at once, and a good number always died.

No wonder! Nobody but Newbold could have ranged cattle at all on the remainder of that mangy range. We used to say that he gave his cows a college course in gleaning, and that a Newbold yearling would gallop half a mile for a blade of grass and run three days for a drink. There wasn't much exaggeration in the second remark, either.

Somebody with a mean nature, plus a sense of humor, gave Newbold his start by making him a donation of his first ledge of the range. That was when he was sixteen. That land raised nothing but coyotes and a few foxes, and even the foxes were out of luck in the district. A bear will dine on anything, from roots to grubs and wasps' nests, but self-respecting grizzlies simply broke down and cried when they had a look at Newbold's gift of land.

But Newbold didn't cry.

He was raised with the silver spoon, at that. Old Man Newbold had made a fortune in lumber, another in cows, another in gold dust, and still another in land. But he used it all on high living and faro. He used to work up a faro system every year or so, and then he would go on a big campaign, but the faro always won. Take it by and large, faro always will. It beats the white men, and it beats the crooks.

So the old man died and left one son and heir; and that boy, who had been raised soft and high, was chucked out into the world with nothing much but hope to fill his poke. Then, as I was saying, an old friend of his father's gave the kid a wedge of desert that was already overcrowded by a fox, a coyote, and half a dozen rabbits, all sinews and fur.

But Newbold took the gift with thanks. He started with about a cow and a half and a burro, by way of live stock. And when big outfits were driving back and forth across the range, and lost young cows and yearlings going across the boy's sun-blasted land, he picked up those dying cattle for half the price of their hides, and then, as we all said, nursed them with pain and promises until they could walk.

I think that cows were afraid to die on Newbold's hands; they had an idea that the earthly paradise was anywhere off his range, and they kept fighting and fixing their sad eyes on the future until they graduated and got to the butcher at last.

Yes, Newbold progressed so rapidly that when he was eighteen he fixed his eyes on more of that range. He took a trip clear to Chicago and walked in on the fellow who happened to own the rest of Hell-on-earth. When this man heard that Newbold wanted to buy, he looked him over and saw that he was all brown steel, like a well-oiled engine. He offered to rent him the range for about a dollar a year, but finally he sold it for something around a dollar an acre, which was sheer robbery, except for the green western valleys, which I have spoken of before.

So Newbold went back west again and got him some

more batches of cows that had used up their first chance in life down to the last half-drop. And from year to year he walked his skeletons back and forth across his range, and lost a lot of them, but made a heap of money on the rest.

He took that range when he was sixteen. He expanded it when he was eighteen. And for fifteen years he raked in dollars off the rocks and blow-sands. In a good, fat country, I don't think he would have done so well. He was one of those geniuses who know best how to make something out of nothing. He was a cactus among men.

At thirty-three, he looked forty-five. He was the hardest heart, and hardest driver, and the meanest boss in the world. He fed worse and paid less than any other outfit. But still he always managed to keep a crew together. In the first place, he was straight; in the second place, he treated himself worse than he treated his men; in the third place, he backed up his boys as though they were his blood brothers when they had a falling out with sheep-herders, or any other poachers; and in the fourth place, and, most important of all, any puncher who could say that he had lasted out a whole year with Newbold was sure to get a job wherever he cared to roll down his blankets and pick out a string.

The fourth reason was the one that brought me to his place. That, and because I had heard of him since I was a youngster, first as "the boy cattle king," and secondly as "that hard case, Newbold."

He was a hard case, all right. His only relaxation was a fight, and even in that line he didn't get much relaxation after a time. He became too well known. Now and then somebody who wanted to make a reputation went up to the ranch and looked for trouble, but that man either turned up his toes on the spot or had to be shipped out for a long list of repairs.

It got so that Newbold would ride sixty miles to wrangle with a neighbor or to take up a remark that somebody else had said somebody else had heard about him. But even these long rides finally began to bring him in very short returns; and all that Newbold could do was to fight the weather, and the prices, and the railroads—three things that even Newbold couldn't beat. Even so, he just about got a draw, as a rule.

9

I think it was because he was running out of trouble, except enough to kill five ordinary men, that he finally thought of raising hay in the western valleys of the range.

It was one of those paper schemes. You sit down with a map and draw a lot of lines. You fence in a lot of the best ground, and then you buy mowing machines and rakes, and you cut the crop, and cure it for hay, and you make a road through the passes, and when the eastern range is as bare as grandfather's red head, then you have a lot of first-rate feed to stuff into the cows and pull them through until the next quarter-inch rain comes along and washes more mud and a little water into the tanks.

That was the scheme of our boss. A good, big scheme. And a scheme that might do wonders. The trouble was, in the first place, that fence building, and road making, and mowing machines, and two-horse rakes, cost money.

However, Newbold struck in on the scheme, and he did it in the true Newbold way. You would think that he would just sit down and write off an order to a big manufacturer of agricultural implements, and pretty soon we would go down to the railroad station and debark, a trainload of everything, covered with shining new blue, and red, and green paint.

But Newbold didn't do that. He was ten miles too mean for that. First he got a one-legged machinist, and a seventy-year-old blacksmith, both of them willing to work for board and tobacco, so to speak. Then he put up a bow-legged shed, and he went away from the ranch on a three weeks' trip.

All through the West, now and again a big farmer or rancher dies and his family splits up, and the first thing that is done is to sell off all the implements. As soon as the paint is rubbed off a gang plow or a mowing machine, it's old. And as soon as it's old, it's not wanted. It may have been worked six months or sixteen years. That doesn't matter. It's simply old. I've seen a hundred-and-twenty-five-dollar mowing machine sell for five dollars, and a forty-dollar subsoil plow sell for one dollar, and a seventy-five-dollar running gear for a wagon auction off for seventy-five cents, and a five-hundred-pound heap of iron junk—chains, hammer-heads, haimes, plowshares— knocked down for a dollar and a quarter. Even junk dealers are not interested when it comes to bidding in on farm wreckage.

Well, Newbold was not proud, in that way. He went out and collected. He attended half a dozen sales, and first of all, up came a forge and a lot of blacksmith's tools, and that sort of thing. And then we got an order to break mustangs to collar and harness; and we went down to the station and began to haul junk forty miles overland to the ranch. It was a long job, and a mean one, and those mustangs could kick off their harness faster than school kids can shed their clothes on the rim of the swimming pool.

But there was the whole mass and heap of stuff, at last. And first of all, he set to work at the forge under the tutelage of the blacksmith of seventy years; and the more intelligent of us—I was not one—were put under the one-legged machinist. He and the blacksmith, do you see, were to supply the brains, and we punchers were the hand power! It was a mean scheme, but then, Newbold was always mean. It was a cheap scheme, but Newbold was always cheap.

We worked for weeks straightening the knock-knees of wagons that had developed flat feet and rheumatism a generation before. We patched harness with secondhand rivets, rawhide, and baling wire. We took out the mysterious insides of mowing machines, and operated, and put them back again, praying all together. We unrolled miles of knotted, tangled, spliced, and rotten secondhand barbed wire. And a roll of barbed wire can play as many tricks as an outlaw mustang, and buck as high, and hit as hard, and bite as deep. Besides, it never gets tired.

But, to make it short, finally we fenced, and plowed, and sowed, and cut, and raked, and windrowed, that land and the hay crop from it.

And then the boss saw that we could never haul that hay in the loose clear across the passes over the so-called road that he had made. He had to get a machine and bale it.

And that was where the trouble started.

Chapter Two

Well, we got a fourth-hand device called a hay press. The name of it was Little Giant.

But it was misnamed. It wasn't little. It was a full-grown giant when it came to making trouble. It had to be a giant, because it succeeded where everything else had failed.

Newbold had not really minded the stretch of trouble that he called a cow range. He liked it. The harder the fight, the more he was pleased; the longer it lasted, the better grew his second wind. Climate or no climate, rain or no rain, prices or no prices, he raised cows, he made men herd them, and he coined money.

And that's why I saw that the hay press was a real giant, because, single-handed, it licked Newbold. It put him on his back. And he was a new man when it got through with him.

I never quite understood the workings of that machine. When he got it, it looked like a cross between a traveling crane and a moving van. It was these things, and something more. It had all the faults of everything, and none of the virtues. It broke the heart of the machinist, and it nearly killed the poor old blacksmith. I shall never forget how he used to sit with his head in one hand, and a broken piece of iron fixture in the other, too tired to swear, and too worried to sleep.

I remember right well the day that we finally hauled the hay press through the worst of the pass, having pried and prayed it over jutting rocks, through tight squeezes, mile after mile. We had chucked stones under the wheels in time to keep it from lurching forward down a slope and crushing the mustangs which hauled it. We had thrown a log under it in time to keep the obstinate fool of a thing from running backward into a ravine. I remember the day for these reasons, and because that was when a pinto beast working in the swing clipped me on the point of the hip with a well-aimed kick just as I was jumping out of range; but most of all, I remember it because that evening a man rode into our camp and sat down to eat with the boys.

He was Dug Waters, whom most people in those days called "White Water," for a lot of obvious reasons. Mostly because, here and there, he had made as much noise and done as much damage as a river at the flood. He was a tall, gentle-looking man with a good deal of Adam's apple, and an embarrassed smile. He had a way of crowding into corners and seeming to beg every one not to notice him.

But the boss noticed him, you can bet.

That fellow Newbold always had a good look at any stranger who sat down to eat his meat in our camp. As I said before, it was the worst chuck that ever was put before cow-punchers, and Heaven knows that cow-punchers never got much of the cream, no matter where they hung their bridles and tried to call home. But Newbold could watch a penny in the shape of sour dough as closely as a jeweler could watch a fine diamond.

At the table was where we liked him least.

He hauled up to where Waters was sitting and asked him his name and business, and when he found out that it was White Water himself, the boss almost choked. He told Waters to start for the sky line as soon as possible, and that the shortest road would probably be the smoothest. He said that he had never turned an honest man from his door, but that he would walk ten miles and swim a river to take the hide of a skunk.

Now, our boss was a known man, but so was Waters, for that matter; and the moment we heard his name and saw how quiet he was, we knew that he was really a dangerous fighter. I've never seen it fail. A fellow of many words never has so many bullets in his magazine. The quiet fellows who seem to think their way from word to word are the ones who wreck a saloon when the time comes, and shoot the tar out of a whole sheriff's posse when they're pursued.

Now, White Water was exactly that sort of a fellow, to judge by the look of him, and to listen to his reputation; but he didn't pull a gun on Newbold. Yet I've never seen more cold poison than there was in the eye that he turned on the boss.

Finally he said:

"Newbold, I'm a sick man. I'm bound on a long journey, and I haven't eaten a morsel for two days. I'll tell you one thing more. I'm not begging on my own account, altogether. I'd see you hanged before I'd do that. But I'm asking you to let me sit here and eat a square meal. I haven't a penny to pay you, but I'll give you the bridle off my gelding, yonder. I can ride him just as well with a halter."

We all watched the boss pretty carefully at this. And I think that almost any other man in the world would have thrown up his hands when he heard and saw the straightness with which White Water was speaking. But Newbold was all chilled steel. He was the stuff that they put in the nose of armor-piercing shells.

"Your bridle and you be danged together," he said. "Get out of this camp before I throw you out! You're a thug, and a thief, and a gunman, and I hate your breed. If you're sick, you're not as sick as I'd like to make you. I'd like to see you and your whole breed drop and the buzzards start on you before your eyes were dark. Now, start along before I use my hands on you!"

I thought that it would be guns, then, and a mighty neat fight, because it made no difference to the boss. Perhaps he preferred fists, but he was just as much at home with knives, or guns, or clubs, even, for that matter. It was a sight to see him there with the red light shaking from the fire over his long, lean, loose-coupled body.

But Dug Waters only looked up at him for a moment as though he were seeing a game bird, away off in the sky. Then he surprised us a good deal by saying:

"You don't have to throw me out. I'll go."

With that he got up and left us, and the amazing part of it was that not one of us, in speaking of the thing afterward, thought that Waters was yellow. We all agreed that he must have had something on his mind. Pete Bramble said that he saw Waters stagger as he raised his foot to the stirrup to go off. And every one of us agreed that he had told the truth and was a sick man. He had the white look of a fellow with very little blood in his body—very little good blood, at least.

And Pete Bramble, after the boss had rolled into his

blankets, looked around him at the silent circle of us and said:

"That's gunna bring us bad luck. That's going too far. When a man's sick—" He stopped and puffed at his pipe.

The cook was standing there in his shirt sleeves, the fire shining on his greasy, red arms.

"When a man's sick?" he echoed. "No, but when he's hungry! Ay, or even a dog, when it's gaunted all up!"

I think he was the worst cook in the world, but I loved him for saying that. We all did. For two or three days hardly a man cursed him for the way he made the coffee or burned the beans.

The next day we got the hay press down to its first location and set her up. It's a hard thing to describe a hay press. In the first place, it's a job I don't like. The less I have to think about them, the better pleased I am. In the second place, I never understood them, and I never wanted to.

But I can say that this thing that turned big hay into small, so to speak, was a long box set upon one end, with a beater in it that worked up and down on long irons. The power that worked it came from four sweating mustangs that scratched their way around and around on a circle, hitched to a beam. Halfway around the circle they were lugging to pull the beater up; the other half they were lugging to jam the feed down. And it was run, run, run for them except when the bale was made, and then the power driver yelled "Bale!" and dropped an anchor board that held the power beam in place until the bale was tied with wire.

The first thing that we did was to start out a fleet of four Jackson bucks. For the benefit of punchers who never saw a Jackson buck, I'll say that it's a thing with a lot of iron-shod and pointed wooden spears that stick out in front. Two horses work behind this line of spears with a wooden, open bulwark in front of them, and behind them sits the driver on a seat that has a single plowwheel under it.

It was my job, at first, to drive one of those Jackson bucks. I admired the contraption a good deal, right at first, but I used up my admiration plenty before the day was an hour old. The trick was to start out with the teeth of the machine hoisted, and while running empty, like that, the

15

clumsy brute was sure to start sliding on a down slope where there was no down slope to see, or zigzagging over bumps where there were no bumps to find. And I ask any cow-puncher to imagine what a pair of broncos only half broke to the saddle and a quarter broke to harness would do with that sort of a stall on wheels weaving around them.

They kicked, and bucked, and threw themselves down, and reared to throw themselves backward, and then they started to run away. But the cards were stacked against those broncs. They were tied in front, and they were tied behind, and they were framed in on both sides, and when they tried to bolt, I just lowered the spears into the ground, and after they had plowed an acre or so, they admitted that they were beat.

So was I. I was kind of chafed a little, to tell the truth. I thought that riding for years in a saddle had given me an outside lining as tough as leather, but I was all wrong. That iron seat on top of that jolting, jouncing, jarring plowwheel found all sorts of new and tender places that I didn't know were on the map.

Finally, the broncs were convinced that it was no good, so I started their work, which was to pick up as many shocks of hay as the buck would hold without spilling and shove them up to the back end of the hay press. The broncs would ram the load home well enough, but when it came to backing up, they couldn't understand. They simply balked. Pete Bramble lighted matches and burned off their chin whiskers before it dawned on them that there were two ways of going, and one of them was back.

But still, it was a hard job. Between pulling my arms out of joint to back my ornery team of nags, and trying to steer that danged sidewheeling invention, and being bumped like a hiccupping rubber ball until my heart and stomach changed places and my liver and lungs got scrambled together, I was ready to quit by noon.

So I went up to the boss to tell him my idea, and there I had my first sight of the kid.

I have to take a new breath before I start talking about him.

Chapter Three

This kid was about fifteen, I should say, very big for his age, and with a pair of smooth shoulders—the sort you see in a well-made mule. He looked more, but you could see that the bull was only beginning to appear in his neck and the mastiff in his jaw, and the mischief in his eye. His face was covered with bright-red freckles.

"They're the sparks and the coals of fire that come out of the top of his head," said Pete Bramble, one day.

For his hair was just the color of fire—red fire. This pug-nosed boy was sitting on a rock chewing a straw and looking like a simpleton, which is a talent that no grown man can divide with a fifteen-year-old brat. He had on about half a hat, with his red hair burning up through the holes in the roof. He had on a shirt that was minus a collar and one sleeve. His trousers were a sawed-off pair that once had fitted a man, and a big man at that. His feet were bare, and so were his calves, with white marks on them where the thorns had scratched.

Take him all in all, he looked like a young mountain lion with the fur peeled off and the hide tanned.

I looked at this young limb for a while, and then I sashayed up to the boss. He gave me the nearest relation to a smile that could be found in his house—about a fifth cousin, say.

"How is things, Joe?" says he.

"Kind of monotonous," said I.

"Monotonous?" says he.

"Well, chief," said I, "I came up and hunted for your shindig because I heard that there was some action to be found around your place."

"Why, Joe," said he, "I've always aimed to keep the boys amused and with enough to do so they won't have to be rocked to sleep at night. I used to keep minstrels and such to soothe them down, but then I decided that I'd have to look up more for them to do. Matter of fact, I haven't had no complaint like yours since I can remember."

"That's a funny thing," said I, "and I'll bet you ain't been keeping your ear peeled close to the ground. Well, it hasn't been so bad, mostly. Breaking in ten-twelve trained outlaws that you call range ponies every year was one pleasin' feature that we all looked forward to, especially me."

"I always guessed that you did, Joe," says the boss. "You look so plumb graceful in the air."

"There was other good features, too," says I. "Like drinking tank water when the wriggles have to be strained out of it and vinegar mixed in; and eating beans twenty-one times a week; and exercising our jaws like lawyers on beef that we never could convince. And the ship's biscuit was entertainin', too, because it was a lot of fun to rap a chunk of it on the edge of the table and see the weevils come out and take notice who was callin' at the front door of their old home."

"Why, Joe," said he, "it seems that I've been running a regular vaudeville show to keep you boys amused. I didn't know that I was laying myself out to do that."

"A regular college, too," says I. "Couple of years up here would make a man pretty handy with some of the dead languages, because it's a cinch that your cows don't understand no living tongue. There's some medical trainin', too, because anybody that can nurse your yearlings through one of these winters ought to be able to set up a 'first-rate' practice giving the rich and the old and the feeble another ten years of life."

"That's an angle I never thought of," said he. "I guess that I ought to start to charge admission, and here I've been all the time paying out regular wages."

"It's been a terrible mistake," says I. "The boys all been wanting to speak about it, but you know—some fellows, they break right down when they find that they can't give away a lot of their dough. We all thought that you must be one of that kind."

"I see how it is," says he, a lot more patient than I ever expected him to be. "My mistake is being too big-hearted and generous all the time."

"I hate to tell you," says I. "I hate to complain, but that's the truth. Look at the way you put up a roof over

18

the bunk house with the roof all patterned with holes, like an open-work shirt, so's we could see the stars while we were lying in the bunks. A plain cow-puncher, he don't expect that much care, and thought and trouble on the part of his boss. Though I must admit that it was handy to know when it was raining, and we could always tell when the cows was likely to freeze to death by the way we felt in the bunk house."

"I see it all, now," says he. "I've just been too kind!"

"Chief," says I, "I'm a humble man, and I don't like to complain, but the hard truth has gotta come out. We're a rough lot, and a thick-skinned lot, and we have to be treated that way. Still, for the sake of education, and all that, I've stuck along on the job, but today is too much. There ain't enough to do on that Jackson Creek to keep me awake."

"Joe," says he, "you fair make my heart bleed. Sitting there on that soft iron seat has sort of culled you."

"Yes," says I, feeling my way along, "about half a yard of hide has been culled right off me. And a fellow like me that has been used to riding thoroughbreds out of Thunder and sired by Lightning, you can't expect him to have his hands full with nothing but a pair of those pets that I've been driving all morning."

"They've been too well taught," said he. "I can see that."

"Yes, chief," says I, "the fact is that it ain't hardly possible to keep them from reciting their lessons all day long. They've been marking up a hundred per cent on me all the time!"

"It's hard to bear," says he.

"Yes," says I. "I'm already limping a little. But I've been waiting and hoping that I would have something to do to keep my hands full and my mind occupied, but the only other thing that I've had has been a three-wheeled cartoon of a wagon that already knows a lot more than I'll ever learn. It can find its way where I never would guess that there is one. That's what I call a college-grad-uate wagon."

"I've been admiring it myself," said he. "And what's the conclusion that you're drifting all these ideas toward, Joe?"

"It's a sad thing, chief," says I, "but I'm going to

19

vamose. I'm afraid that you've got the wrong kind of man in me. You oughta fill up your bunch with recruits from the old folks' home, or a hospital, or something like that; the sort of people that wouldn't ask to be more than just mildly occupied and amused for about twenty hours a day, the way I've been. You take old people, and they get childish again, and they don't mind lying down and sleeping right through the whole of four or five hours a night."

"Old son," says he, "I see that you're giving me the best advice in the world. I thank you, and I'm mighty grateful to you. But I can't help suggesting that maybe I could shift your berth and give you another job."

"What job?" said I. "What sort of a job on this Christmas Eve knitting party?"

"Why, there's the forking and feeding job," said he. "Pete Bramble has been pretty nearly going to sleep on his feet, over there with the Jackson fork. Why not change with him?"

"I dunno that Pete would want to change," said I.

"I've got kind of an idea," says he, "that Pete would actually change with anybody. Even the wire cutter, over yonder."

This wire cutting was a job that I hadn't looked into much, so far, but I could hear a good deal from this fellow who was running the outfit there; sometimes the sound of him half a mile away went into my mustang like a whip and made him jump.

Here speaks up the red-headed kid.

"That wire-cutting job was made for me," says he.

The boss looks him over.

"Ain't you too old for that kind of active work?" says he.

"I'm getting kind of childish again," says the kid. "I just want to stand around and play with toys like that all day."

"You know all about hay presses, I guess?" says the boss.

"No, not all about 'em," says the boy. "I've forgot a lot. But I used to build 'em. That's all."

"D'you think," says the boss, "that you could cut as many wires in three hours as we can use in one?"

"I think," says the kid, "that I could cut as many wires in one hour as you could use in three."

"I guess you could," says the boss, with a sneer. "I guess you could do that. I guess you're a regular dollar-a-day man, ain't you?"

"You know the way the saying goes?" said the kid. "Put up or shut up!"

Newbold jumped a little. Then he remembered that he was only talking to a kid. He looked at that boy again, up and down.

"Kid," said he, "go over and do your stuff. Tell Bosh Miller that he can step down from that wire stretcher."

The boy still sat where he was and chewed on the straw and twisted it slowly from one side of his mouth to the other.

"At a dollar per?" said he.

"If you can turn out as many wires as we use. Yes!" says the boss. "But if you spoil more than two of those wires— What's your name?"

"Chip," says the boy.

"If you spoil more than two of those wires, I'll make you less than a sliver," said the boss.

But he was talking to the dust that lad made as he streaked it for the wire cutter.

"Now, Joe, what are you saying?" remarks the boss to me.

"Well," I said, "if Pete Bramble is chump enough to want to change jobs with me, I suppose that I'm chump enough to want to stay on and see how the thing turns out. That kid's a whale!"

So I sauntered over to the stack and asked Pete if he wanted to change to my job.

He came blinking to me through a cloud of dust. He took me by both shoulders.

"Boy," said he, "d'you mean it?"

"Sure," says I.

He said not a word. He simply turned and climbed for the spot where my buck was standing. I looked down at my shoulders. There was a stain of blood on each of them.

Chapter Four

It's a strange fish that can swim out of water; and the trouble with the whole business was that while Newbold knew all about cows, he did not know all about hay presses. Not half! He had a theory, and theories have wrecked greater men than Newbold.

A theory is the sort of thing that takes ten dollars, and sells on a margin when the market is climbing, and pyramids all the way, and makes three hundred and twenty dollars the first week, and ten thousand the second, and three hundred and twenty thousand the third, and ten million the fourth, and three hundred and twenty million the fifth, and ten billion the sixth—and there you are!

The seventh week that theory has the multimillionaires and all that small-time crowd asking for introductions; and the eighth week they beg for jobs, and the authorities vote a medal to the Napoleon of finance who kindly didn't take up the whole of Wall Street and the rest of the country into the bargain.

Right at the beginning, Newbold showed us his theory. He says:

"The shorthorn who sells me this machine, he says that it bales forty-five tons a day, and averages forty, because you gotta waste a little time taking it down, and moving it, and setting it up again. Now, we'll allow five tons a day of lying to that crook. Still, we've got an average of thirty-five tons a day. We've cut three thousand acres, and we ought to bale twenty-five hunderd or three thousand tons; and we ought to do that in ninety days. Now, ninety days is a lot of time, but so is three thousand tons a lot of feed. It ought to feed five thousand weak head of cows for a hundred days of the worst winter or the worst summer pickings. You see what that would mean to us."

He always put it that way. He was always talking as though we were a company in which he was no more than the executive officer, say.

This same fellow who sold him the machine had said that the right pay was eighteen cents a ton to the bale roller, seventeen cents a ton to the feeders, and fourteen cents to the power driver.

But the chief did not remember that much of the talk. Only later we found out. What the chief offered us was just half of the right rates. However, even that looked pretty fat to us.

You take eight cents a ton, say, for forty tons a day, and you've got three dollars and twenty cents of any man's money. And that makes close onto a hundred a month if you don't knock off for Sundays.

And would we knock off? We would not! We lay around in our bunks, that first night, and we bought ourselves new saddles, and picked up thoroughbreds for a song, and won the Kentucky Derby with them, and took trips to New York and Cuba, and just raised heck in general.

Even the kid had done his share, and more than his share. He had hopped around from one end of that machine to the other and actually cut a lot more wires than the machine had managed to use up. He kept the wire fairly jumping off the coil, and the head-twister warm, he hummed it around so fast. We used a big wire for the central part of the bale, and a smaller wire for the ends. He could make the thinner variety fairly hop off the machine of its own volition. The bigger kind he had to strain over, bracing his weight to get down the stretching lever. But he never said no, and his production was steady all afternoon.

At the end of the day he goes up to the chief as fresh as paint and says:

"You gotta be congratulated on having one first-class man, Newbold."

"Which man is that?" asks Newbold.

"Me," says the kid. "If you don't believe it, look at that!"

And he pointed back to a fine little stack of wires which he had cut and laid out. Nowbold usually had a word when he wanted one, but this time he was plainly beat. He had to turn around and walk off, and that kid got on at a steady job with a man-sized salary of a dollar a day, which was real pay, in those days.

But I have to leave the kid, for a time, and get back to what was happening to the hay press.

The job of forking from the stack looked all right, and it sounded all right. All you had to do was to grab that three-cornered Jackson fork and plant it in a wad of hay. Then you yelled "Hey!" and the derrick driver started up his horse and jerked that load up into the air. And when it was dangling over the feed platform, you pulled the trip line and the load dumped down where the feeder could get at it. It looked easy. You seemed to be standing around a lot of the time, doing nothing.

But it didn't turn out so easy.

For a starter, the fork weighed forty pounds, and all those pounds were put in the worst places. There were four long, curved teeth, needle-pointed, and always trying to get at your legs with a down-drop of a side flip, or some other dodge. And the trip iron had a sharp edge and was specially designed to clamp down over your fingers.

Then there was an art in using that fork. On the one hand, you had to dodge the spears of bucks as they came steaming in with all the push of two-mustang power behind them. And then as you side-stepped, you heard the feeder screeching at you for more hay. But you had to put in the fork just so. If you didn't use the fork so that it divided the big, snarled masses a little, the feeder had to break his back muscling it apart. And if you tried to help the feeder by sending up small forkfuls, you half killed the derrick horse, which had to back up, all the time; and, in addition, you starved the feeder you were trying to help. Add to all this that you worked in a cloud of thick dust and chaff that filled your neck, and your throat, and your eyes, and it makes a pretty picture. But not strong enough for the fact. Nothing is as strong as the facts about a hay press, no matter how words are put together.

Well, I got through that afternoon, and when I came to the end of the working day—which was about dark, and long after sunset—I was almost too tired to wash my hands.

Then I waddled into the cook house along with the rest, and while I was looking at the greasy flapjack and sowbelly which the cook called our supper, and trying to make a start in eating, in came the chief, with hay burs sticking

24

out of his hair and chaff down his back, stuck to his flannel shirt.

He had been adding up the tags of the bale roller, and he was pretty sour.

Then he said: "Nineteen goldarned tons!"

"Nineteen tearin' wild cats!" said I.

The chief sat down at his plate, and looked at the flapjacks, and turned his head, and opened his mouth to say something to that red-armed clown of a cook. But he seemed to remember in time that he was the man who bought the food the poor cook had to eat, and that stopped his mouth for him a little.

Nineteen tons!

It was right. He showed us the books, and nobody would believe, and everybody took a look. Our bales were averaging about a hundred and eighty pounds, and we had only turned out a little more than two hundred of them. The feeders swore that they had pitched at least a thousand tons of blankety-blank hay down the throat of the what-not press; and the bale roller said they lied like something else, because he, personally, had taken out at least two thousand tons, and had tied, tagged, and rolled, and piled it.

Just then up speaks the kid.

Those greasy flapjacks didn't bother him a bit. He ate them as though they were sponge cake and the sowbelly was honey. And he floated down his food with the alkali solution which our cook called coffee.

Says the kid:

"You know how it is, boys. You gotta learn. If I was up there on that feeding platform, I'd show you how to build your first feed big, and then taper them off so's the last one is just a kick of your foot to knock some chaff down the throat of the old lady."

We all looked at him. For my part I wanted to throttle him. The old man says:

"You know, do you?"

"Sure I know!" says the kid. "I used to build these here machines. You might say I invented 'em."

"Well," said the chief, "tomorrow morning you're gunna climb up there onto the platform and show us. And you ain't going to come down till noon."

"Aw, that's all right," says the kid.

25

But he looked a little startled.

We dropped the beater in that mankiller at four sharp in the morning, and sure enough, there was the kid up there, with a pitchfork taller than his head.

And when he had said that he knew, he was right! You could drown him with a forkload of hay that crammed the platform to the far corners, but somehow or other he would manage to clear the feed table, and when it raised its ugly long lower jaw, sure enough there was a full bite for its long, square throat to swallow.

He built the first feed high and thick, and sloped it off, and packed it on top; and when the beater rose to the top of its height, he gave the upper layers of the feed a shove with the fork and started the load sliding even before the table rose. And so he poked a starter that nearly choked the press and got the bale well started.

And he could pick to pieces a tangle of hay that looked like a trail problem built up out of barbed wire. And even when the feed floor looked as bare as the flat of your hand, he seemed able to pick out another feed for the making bale out of the corners, here and there. But, all the time, he was riding me, out there on the stack, and calling down to me to find out if I was asleep, and how long had I been off baby food, and wasn't I only part of a man, and when was the rest of the sandwich coming?

He not only had tongue for me, but he used to stir up the derrick driver, too. That driver was an Irishman by the name of Clive Rooney, and once Rooney started to climb up to the feeding platform and take the boy apart; but the kid stood right there and dared him to come on and told him he would straighten his crooked jaw for him and knock a whole vocabulary down his throat.

This line of talk cleared Rooney's head a little, and he remembered that he was dealing with a mere kid. So he went back to his single-tree and derrick horse; but with every trip that the horse made out and back, Rooney gave one black look at the kid up there on the table.

It wasn't Rooney alone, or I, that tasted the boy's tongue. Sometimes he leaned around the corner of the press and asked the power driver if he had a team of prairie rabbits, or were they just burros; and he got that fellow to raging and throwing the whip into the ponies.

And still the brat had time to lean over the edge of

26

the table and tell the bale roller a few things, and ask him if he thought he was rolling dice, and if he hoped to bale more than he could eat, and who had told him he was old enough to leave home.

He even had a few words for the drivers of the bucks, and the squeak of his voice cut clear and high through all the clangor of the press, and the cursing and shouting of the men.

After a while, he stopped bothering me. I guess he saw that I wasn't to be made angry. And the fact is that I was too interested in watching his tactics to lose my temper. For he was playing the gadfly and driving the whole set of us, grown men though we were. He wanted us to bale hay, and he was making us do it.

Also, I could not help wondering how long he would last. He could not keep up the pace till noon, I knew. It was very plain that Chip knew all about feeding, and that he knew all the art of handling a pitchfork—for it is an art—but in spite of his craft, and his strength beyond his years, and his wild spirit, he simply could not stand there in the flying dust with the temperature a hundred in the shade—Heaven knows what it was in the sun fire and hay smoke where he was working—and push so many tons into the feed box forever.

We worked from four to six. Then we had breakfast. At breakfast, the kid was as gay as a lark, and taunting all of us; at ten o'clock we had a lunch of stewed prunes, bread, and coffee. The kid was still pretty chipper, but not quite so gay. He didn't come down from the platform. He simply sang out:

"What's the matter? You boys think you're all at school and are getting paid for your recess time?"

He didn't come down. He just disappeared, and I knew that he had flopped down flat on the table to rest there, in spite of the beating of the sun.

I finished off my lunch before the rest and sneaked a cup of coffee up to the platform. He was dead to the world, his eyes closed, his mouth hanging open. I shook him by the shoulder, and he got up with a start.

He gave me one hard look, tossed off the coffee, handed the cup back to me, and said not a word. He just got up and grabbed his pitchfork again.

I went back to the cook house and threw in the cup.

27

I said: "You'd best call down the kid from the feed table, chief. Or he'll kill himself before noon."

"Let him kill himself, then!" says the boss, and Rooney and a couple more chimed in with the same idea.

So I went back to watch, and to worry. For I began to guess that I'd said more than I knew, and come closer to the truth.

Chapter Five

Believe it or not, between four in the morning and eleven, that lad shifted fourteen tons from the feeding table into the feed box.

A whisper of this went around, and even the hard hands on that crew wanted to see the kid let off. Marvel or no marvel, of course he couldn't keep on at that rate. Not at fifteen years of age. Only, I want to repeat that he didn't look quite as young as fifteen. I want to say that for us all. We knew that we were doing something bad; we didn't know really how bad.

But when eleven o'clock came and the boy was still at work up there on the platform, I was outright worried.

He had stopped all of his pestering talk, by this time. Through the rifts of the dust-smoke, I could see his face set and lined like the face of an old man. He was taking his punishment and never making a murmur. I don't suppose it had occurred to him that there could be a man in the world like our chief, with a mind as small as an arrowhead, and a heart as hard!

The sun went higher, and kept pouring down a billion tons of yellow-white, scalding sunshine. We changed the power horses every hour. We changed the bale rollers every two hours. But the kid was still up there in the swelter of that furnace, never ready to say die!

Poor Chip!

Then Fate came along and offered him an ace from the bottom of the deck.

I mean, Miss Marian Wray came cantering up on her

best saddle horse. It was a good deal of a surprise, though the Wray place was no more than ten miles away, which couldn't be called any distance at all. But you wouldn't expect Marian Wray to be that far away from home—not hardly with a company of troops for an escort, to say nothing of being all by herself.

For she was the real silver spoon, Back Bay, how d'you do aristocrat. She made me pretty sick, the way that she went around with her chin in the air.

I don't mean to say that she snubbed anybody. She was the opposite to that. She was always friendly, and never let anybody go by without saying a few words, and the boys were crazy about her. But for my part, I never liked a peaches-and-cream, picture-book blonde. I never liked them a bit, and I liked Miss Marian Wray the least of the lot, with her democratic manner.

She even used to go to the dances, now and then. But she never stayed more than thirty-one minutes. Thirty minutes to stand around and admire the decorations, and say that things were "too sweet," and the decoration committee had sure outdone itself, and that sort of rot. And then for one minute she slid out onto the floor with "Tex" Brennan, or somebody like that, that knew how to step, and made all the rest of the girls look like zero minus.

The funny thing about it was that the other girls didn't seem to see through it, either. And the whole dang countryside, when you mentioned Marian Wray, just broke down and gibbered, and practically wrung its hands over her, and the women were as bad as the men. I suppose that they thought she was so rich and lovely and beautiful and everything that's to be desired that there was no use in even envying her.

She was all dressed up like a regular range girl, with a broad-brimmed hat and a loose blouse, and divided skirts, and the look of her blowing along in the wind of the gallop was enough, I have to confess, to make a fellow's heart jump.

But when she came up close, she was a lot more Back Bay than range. She had a tailored and a manicured look, as though three maids had been working all morning to turn her out like this.

Even the boss was staggered a little by the arrival of

29

the girl. All the other men were hanging out their tongues, they were so anxious to hear two words spoken by this queen of the May. And even the chief almost took a few minutes off.

I say "almost," but not quite. He just used the interval while the power horses were being changed, to chat with her, and all those grown-up fools of men craned their necks at that girl, and admired her, and grinned at her, and looked blushing and stupid, and ready to drop dead if she ever said the word.

"I see that you're a great natural innovator, Mr. Newbold," she said.

"Oh, I had a little idea. That's all," says Newbold.

And he grinned at her, too, wide and simple as any of the rest.

I bit off a hunk of tobacco from the corner of my plug, and while I worked it into a comfortable spot in the hollow of my face, and felt the cheek muscles pulling soft and easy over the point of the load, I looked that girl over and wondered a little at what soft-heads we men are. Because most days she would have hit me just as hard as she always hit all the rest. But that day I was too worried about the boy, and the perspiration in my eyes and the chaff down my neck. I couldn't have been romantic for a thousand dollars a minute, paid in advance.

I just looked that girl over and said to myself: "Bunk! Give me something with a commoner look, because you'll wear old sooner than any of the rest."

She was going around and admiring everything. It was the first time she ever had seen a hay press in action. I heard her telling the power driver how terribly brave he must be to be out there behind those dashing, crashing horses, because suppose the beam should break, what would happen to him when it kicked back?

And she said to the bale roller how could anybody really do so many things at once, and wasn't it wonderful how the human hand could work as if an independent brain were operating in it. Then she came back and gave me a look and she said what a frightful peril I was in, handling those four sharp, crooked, lancelike things. She called me Joe, too, because that was her idea. Look at Napoleon. He knew the name of all the men in his army, didn't he?

Well, that was her trick. So doggone queenly that the meanest of her subjects was good enough to get a glad eye from her.

"You bet your boots, if you're wearing boots," said I, "that it's a frightful peril—"

And I was about to add something else, when the dust cloud blew away from the feed platform and she saw the white face of the kid just as he sank his pitchfork into a wad of hay bigger than himself, a good deal.

"Great heavens, Mr. Newbold," she sings out, with something in her voice that sent the pickled chills even up my back, "do you employ children—at cut wages?"

Did he employ children!

I thought that Newbold wanted the earth to open and swallow him, and I wished that it would, and never let him out again.

Chapter Six

It was not often that one had a chance to see the great Newbold put down. But down he was now. Just then that ornery boy, Chip, leans out from the table, after shoving down the last feed on a bale, and just as the driver yells "Bale!" the kid sings out:

"Hey, Newbold! Is this a dance that we've bought tickets for? Or what are all the skirts around for?"

I thought that Rooney would climb up and massacre that kid, when he heard the remark; and the bale roller leaned his head out after he'd jerked the bale out of the press and locked the door behind it, and gave the kid a glare.

But I understood.

Chip wasn't cashing in on any female sympathy. And it gave my heart a stir. I can tell you, when I saw what an outright man the boy was. I knew that he was sick all the way to the bottom of his boots from the work he had done, but he wasn't complaining! He was willing to leave the women out of the matter!

He said to Marian Wray:

You can imagine that the chief did not waste any time using the kid's lead.

"You see—fresh kid that wants to show us how to run the hay press. I'm taking some of the crow out of the little rooster!"

"I know," says Marian Wray. "Some of them are that way. Gutter ruffians from birth. I suppose one ought to pity the poor little wretches!"

But there wasn't much pity in her, just then. She gave the kid a look that would have melted a galvanized iron roof; but Chip already had his back to her and was jamming a fresh feed down the throat of that old press. He was as game as they came!

He had given Marian Wray something to think about. She gathered the remnants of her usual smile about her—strange how pretty girls all learn to smile like actresses!—and pretty soon off she went.

As soon as she was hull down, I waited for the boss to call poor Chip off the table, and I even saw the boy give the chief one side glance, but Newbold pretended to have forgotten him. There was no mercy in that heart of his. And having cashed in on the boy's pluck and spirit of fair play to get the girl out of the way, Newbold just left him up there to work his heart out.

It seemed to me that every minute would be his last one. I could see the boy wabble and shake as he staggered about. But he continued to stick that pitchfork into the hay; and he continued to heave the hay over into the mouth of the press; and his last bale was as fat and firm all the way through as his first one.

And, finally, the last long hour wore away from minute to minute, with the whole crew of us watching nothing but the fight that boy was putting up.

The fact is that he lasted until the sun was right over our heads, and by twelve, noon, he had shoveled sixteen tons of hay off that platform. I have had a lot of grown men who knew the business doubt the thing, but I was there and saw it done, and I added up the pages in the bale-roller's book with my own fair hand.

It was eighteen pounds over sixteen tons, to be exact. And the boy was fifteen!

As I was saying, he kept right on until the cook banged

32

on a pan at the door of his cook house to show that it was high noon by his stove, no matter what it was by the sun.

So the boys knocked off work, and the derrick and power horses were unhooked, and everybody started wiping chaff out of his shirt collar, and dust out of his eyes. But I watched the kid and saw him start down the side of the press, and then change his mind and come slowly over to the hay dump, which was slanting up to the feed table, half dust, clods, and the rest chaff. He lowered himself over the edge of the table and slid down.

Halfway to the bottom, his body slewed around, like a boat in a running current with nobody at the tiller, and he rolled the rest of the way.

You might have thought that he had given his head an extra hard knock on a lump of sun-fried earth on the way down, but I knew what was the matter.

I ran over and picked him up by the nape of the neck and had a squint at his face. He was blue around the mouth and white around the eyes. He looked like one of those painted monkeys. And he was limp as a dishrag.

So I hauled him over to the drinking water and doused him good and plenty, and dragged him into the shade under the cook house, and hoisted his legs higher than his head, and began to fan him.

The boys came around and helped. They didn't say anything. Not a one of them had anything to offer. But one man took the fold of newspaper out of my hand and continued the fanning, and I remember how Pete took a soaked rag and squeezed out a steady stream of drops onto the hollow of the kid's throat. They were an ugly lot of men. They were ashamed of themselves, and nothing is more dangerous than a man who's ashamed of himself. He wants to get back his self-respect all in one stroke.

Big Newbold came up and said: "Well, the brat's had his lesson, I guess."

Nobody spoke, even then, but every man jack of us turned and gave the boss a good, thoughtful look. He said no more. He cleared his throat and pretended to get interested in the making of a cigarette. But I saw a small white spot in both of his cheeks, and I knew that even Newbold, if he couldn't feel shame, could feel fear, at least.

We worked about a half hour, and still nobody spoke a word, except when one man would call another a chump, with underlinings, and shoulder him out of the way to take up his share of the work. For my part, I had made up my mind that Chip was dying, and that Newbold would be dead soon after, when the kid fluttered his eyelids, and looked at us in a puzzled way, and then sighed and closed his eyes again.

"Mommie!" says he, and turns over on one arm, and sighs again.

It knocked me all in a heap, for some reason. I mean, we didn't need to see his birth certificate, just then, to see that he was two or three years younger than we'd been rating him. If we felt sick before, you can imagine how we felt when we heard him speak, and saw him turn and sigh, like a child in his bed when his mother kisses him good night.

Newbold took hold of me with an iron hand and moved me out of the way and leaned to have a look. He didn't say anything. His face was better than a whole book filled with words.

Just then up pipes a quiet, musical voice, as cold as the snow-water in a mountain stream, and says:

"I see that you allowed him to keep right on showing you how to run the press, Mr. Newbold!"

It was the girl.

Her horse had cast a shoe, and she'd come on back at a walk to see what our camp could do about it, because she knew that we had a good blacksmith attached.

Well, it was the very worst thing that could have happened to us. It was the sort of a story that we would not like to have even men repeat. But as for a woman—why, it was a yarn that every woman in the countryside would eat up, and give forth again with embroideries. And every time the yarn was repeated, our crew would be made to seem more and more like cannibals—child-eaters!

Above all, to have Marian Wray talking about us, and starting the thing! For everything she said would be taken as an under-statement. My first thought was to start right then, horse or foot, and climb for the nearest railroad, and put a thousand miles of 'dobe between me and that scene.

I think that the rest had the same idea.

34

But the first thing we knew, there she was, sitting with the head of the boy in her lap, and not regarding us at all.

She just said: "The poor child! The poor little boy!"

And she ran her thin fingers through his dusty, chaff-filled hair, and brushed it back from his forehead.

This was only a starter. Somehow, she managed to convey that there was a thousand leagues of distance between such a "poor little boy," and grown-up male brutes like us.

Perhaps she was right.

Then, while the iron was hot—melting hot—she said:

"You might stop pouring on the water. His temperature is already subnormal. We might as well try to save what's left of his life." But she added at once: "Though, of course, after the shock of this he'll never be anything but the wreck of a man!"

We didn't question her medical wisdom. It was a case where we felt that she had us with a strangle hold, and the less we said, the better for all of us.

I forgot exactly what she did. But I think that she asked us if we had any whisky, and begged our pardon for suggesting that we might be carrying such poison around with us. Poison? She was the poison, just then. She was poisoning us all. I swear that she even kept a little smile at the corners of her lips. And every now and then she raised her glance from the boy and fixed one or two of us, slowly, carefully, as though she wanted to remember our names and faces for future reference.

Altogether, it was a miserable time. I even forgot to feel any sympathy for the boy. I would rather that he had been run over in a stampede and turned into a patch of fertilizer on the ground than that he should have involved us all so deeply.

Now and then I gave Newbold a look, and after the second or third one, I was amazed to see that even the rhinoceros hide which he wore in the place of a skin had been pierced, and that he was suffering a good deal. Rather more than a good deal!

Finally he said: "Miss Wray, I didn't know—"

She lifted her head, with that ice-cold imitation of a smile.

"You didn't know what, Mr. Newbold?" she asked.

35

He faced her. I must say that for him.

"I didn't know that I could be such a brute!"

I'm sorry to say what followed. She looked him right in the eye and answered:

"Oh, didn't you?"

It was the wickedest remark I've ever heard passed along from one human being to another. And I've heard some pretty active tongues inspired with red-eye, at that.

Just then the boy stirs and groans.

"It's all right," said she. "It's all right now, poor dear!"

At that, the kid sits bolt upright, with a start. He gives a look around, and stares at the girl.

"What's all this kindergarten bunk?" says he. "Cut it out!"

And he got right up on his feet!

Chapter Seven

Well, I must say that it did me a lot of good to see the boy fetch himself up to his feet again. He made a sort of wabbling first step, but he caught hold of himself again and leaned a hand against the rim of a cook-wagon wheel.

"Gimme the makings, Joe, will you?" says he.

I knew by the green of his gills that he didn't want a cigarette. But I fished out the makings and began to roll one for him. I could see that he was making a play to kill time. The rest of the men could see the same thing.

But the girl did not understand. She followed the boy and says to him:

"Don't you think that you'd better lie down again? You really are not as well as you think. Something has happened, my poor boy——"

He gives her a mean look. Then he turns to the rest of us.

"How does she get that way?" says he. "Lead me away from it, Joe, because it might be catching."

It set Miss Wray back quite a few steps to hear these cracks.

But she kept on. When a woman has made up her mind that she's being good, and that she's on the right track, hardly anything will stop her.

"As a matter of fact," says she, "hadn't you better come home with me? My father has need of such a—man—as you are."

She set off that word "man" as a concession, between a couple of her sweetest smiles.

Says the kid: "Who's your old man, ma'am?"

"He's Judge Arthur Wray," says the girl gently, so as not to swamp the poor kid with the full glory of the name.

"Judge Arthur Wray? Judge Arthur Wray?" says the kid, cocking up one eye, as though he had to think hard to remember a name that everybody in the West knew as well as they knew the Tetons. "Oh, yeah. I remember, now. He's the fellow who roped and hog tied the Injuns in that land deal, ain't he?"

Well, it was true, some people said, that old Judge Wray had used more corn whisky than cash to get out of the Indians some of the best rangeland that cows ever grazed.

If it was not a tender point with the Wray family, at least it was plain that the girl had heard about it. She got a sunset-red into her face in no time at all. Perhaps she could have answered, but that terrible kid didn't give her time.

He went right on:

"It might be that your old man wants a good hand on his place. But you tell him I'm mighty grateful, but that I don't talk Injun good enough to be much use to him. And I do talk hay press."

"Of all—" began the girl.

Then she stopped herself. Perhaps she remembered that she was about to say something trite. Perhaps she only cut off something always old but always new.

She just takes a fresh breath, however, and goes ahead. As I was saying, you can't stop a woman when she thinks that she's carrying the flag. She'll keep on carrying it even while she's walking over a thousand faces, grinding in her high heels.

"You'd better think it over. I left my father a few miles back, but we can pick him up on the way. And when I tell him—well, I'm sure that he'll want to employ you. You know that there's room for young—men—to rise with him. He had to go out on a hunt this morning, but I think we'll find him on the way back."

"Hunting Injuns?" asked the boy, who seemed to be all calluses and no tender places.

The girl was patient, and sweet as pie.

"Hunting a thing worse than Indians," says she. "A real criminal, mankiller. A desperado," she winds up. And shakes her head, and smiles again, as though the courage of old Judge Wray staggered her a little.

"What might his monicker be?" says Chip, the tough kid. "What's his name?"

"My father's name?" says she, as patient and angelic as ever.

"No. This here desperado's," says the boy.

"His name," she said, "is Douglas Waters."

"Hold on!" says the boy. "I didn't know you played with a joker in the pack."

"Joker?" says she, a little bewildered.

"You mean," says Chip, "that your old man is out man hunting the squarest shooter, and the best bunkie, and the rightest puncher that ever rode the range? Is that what you mean? Then if I see him, I wouldn't talk about a job, I guess. I'd talk something stronger."

He turns to me:

"Joe," says he, "come on over here and lemme show you something about the way to throw a Jackson fork, will you?"

"Sure," said I.

I got hold of him under the elbow, and he gave me plenty of his weight to pack. And so we walked right out on the well-meaning Miss Wray!

She seemed to be lagging to leeward with most of the wind out of her sails, and I must say that our chief seemed to be swallowing a smile that would have choked a sperm whale.

I didn't talk about Jackson forks. I just rushed the boy over to the shady side of the pile of bales and sat him down there, and then, with my hat, I fanned him.

He leaned back with his arms and legs sprawling, like a hopeless drunk. And his lips kept twitching in and out and up to the sides, like a man who is wondering whether he can last it out or not.

The first thing he said was: "Keep your eye peeled. Don't let 'em see me—like this!"

"You're as right as a trivet," says I. I never knew what a trivet was. But so the saying goes. "Don't you worry," said I. "I'm keeping my eye peeled. If anybody shows, you'll be drawing a design on the ground and teaching me something."

His lips twitched a couple of more times before he managed to smile. And then he took my advice and began to draw lines in the dust. But he put his eye on me for a minute.

"You're a partner, Joe," he gasped. "You're an old partner!"

I wanted him to lie down, until the sick fit passed. But I didn't make the suggestion, because I knew that he wasn't the kind that lies down. You find men like that, one in a million; and boys like that—one in the world.

He preferred to sit up and take his medicine that way. He would rather have been on his feet, I knew.

And, while I watched him fighting out his fight, and beating the game, I looked the boy over, and admired him a good deal more than I know how to say.

And I wondered at him, too, and thought to myself that, after all, boys are foolish when they wish to grow up. If they're strong enough to sight a rifle and ride a horse, they can do most of what men can do. And if they can do these things, they're about as good as men, take it all in all.

Besides that, they have advantages all their own. They're all by themselves. A woman is a woman from the time she is old enough to take a baby doll by the scruff of the neck and call it hers. And a man is a poor, weak, sentimental, sickly servant of the grown woman, their house-builder, jack-of-all-trades, supporter, and royal jester. They reward him by putting a cap and bells on his head, and they give him, as a bauble or scepter, a pretense of admiration for the muscles and the brain power which is always used merely to support the wife and the brats.

A grown man is a grown idiot. That's all. But a boy is different. That's why a boy is the only four-square-to-all-the-winds creature in the world. He goes his own way. He hews to a mark and a line, and lets the chips fall where they may—and he generally hopes that they'll fall in your eye.

And as I sat there, fanning Chip, and admiring him, I couldn't help wondering at the ease with which he had settled beautiful Marian Wray.

She was beautiful. She was lovely enough to take off the top of a man's head. One of her smiles was enough to keep a poor puncher awake at night, turning from side to side, for a month on end. She was so charming that she had taken the crew of the hay press into the hollow of her hand in no time at all. Just a look around had been enough.

But she couldn't take Chip into the hollow of her hand. Not into the hollow of two hands, even. Indeed, she was helpless.

What was all her beauty to him? He would rather have had a shiny new .22 than all of her, ten times over. He would have traded a gross of Marian Wrays for a three-year-old mustang with a kink in its tail and fire in its eye.

So where the rest of the men had been paralyzed, he had walked right in and used his fists, so to speak, on the thin china of which she was made, and he had wrecked her, and blamed her father, and given her something to think about that would keep her turning from side to side for months on end.

Well, boys are a weakness with me. They always have been, and they always will be. I admire them. But when it comes to a show-down, I envy them more than I admire.

But as I sat there and looked at Chip, and thought of his power, and of what he had done that day, and might do again, I couldn't help sighing when I remembered that, within a couple of years, he would be like all the rest of us. The arrow would strike him in the heel; the sweet poison would run through flesh and bone; he would become the same sort of maundering sentimentalist that we all know so well and understand so intimately, because we're the same woman-ridden, adoring, despising caricatures of Samson.

The glory of Chip was sure to pass. He would come to his mortal doom, sooner or later.

But just then, he was complete, independent, sure as a fortified Rock of Gibraltar. And I looked at him as at a sort of super-creature.

Then he began to talk about the Jackson fork.

Chapter Eight

The next three weeks I don't like to think about, and I don't like to write about.

First, the weather got hotter every day, and the hay press broke down every day.

Second, the chief fell in love with Marian Wray, and the hay press broke down every day.

Third, inside of forty-eight hours everybody on that crew hated everybody else, and the hay press broke down every day.

Fourth, and most important of all, the hay press broke down every day.

Taking the things one by one, I have to admit that the middle of the Nevada desert is about as hot as you can wish; but it was cool and crisp compared to the heat that we had out there on that pressing job. The last moisture was sucked out of the hay. You could break the stalks across as though they had been the stalks of straw, after the harvest. And the last moisture was drawn out of the men, also. We were all dry powder, and any word was likely to drop like a spark into a mine. Gun fights were not in order, quite; but I had two fist fights on my own account. The first one was all right; but the second was with Pete Bramble, and we beat each other to a pulp. I got an eye on me that looked like a leather patch, and poor Pete had to talk and eat on one side of his face for days afterward.

But somehow the worst thing that happened, next to the hay press, was the way that the chief fell in love.

"Fell" is the only word for it. He dropped about a mile, straight over the edge, and he landed so hard you could hear the splash.

You see, it appeared that old Judge Wray himself was thinking about buying a hay press, for reasons unlike those of Newbold. Wray's land was so good that his cows simply couldn't eat all the grass that grew, and so he wanted to

41

fence off some sections and raise hay on them. There was plenty of sale for it. So he came over a number of times, and Marian came along with him.

Poor Newbold hardly ever looked at her, but you could tell at a glance what he was thinking about. He was out of his head about half of the time.

I heard them, for instance, talking together one day, and the judge says:

"A coat of paint would save that machine a lot. Put on a good wearing coat of heavy paint and the timbers wouldn't crack in the sun so much. I've got some heavy gray stuff at home—"

"Dark gray," says Newbold, "looking kind of blue in the evening light—"

"Who the deuce cares what it looks like in the evening light?" says Wray. "The bale this turns out—what would you say the weight is?"

"About a hundred and thirty-five, I'd say," says Newbold dreamily.

"What?" says Wray. "I thought you said they'd average closer to two hundred!"

"Oh, you mean the bales," said Newbold.

"What did you think I meant?" asked the judge.

Yes, Newbold was completely knocked over by the pretty face of that girl. Perhaps he was most attracted by his very sense of the impossibility of the thing. For after she knew how he had treated young Chip, her lip curled every time she looked at Newbold.

Not that Chip asked for sympathy from any one. She was scared to death of his active young tongue and never tried anything more than a smile with him after that first day when he let her down so hard.

But the weather, and the wrangling among the crew, and Newbold's stunned look when the girl was around, were all nothing compared to that danged press.

Never could tell what would happen.

Sometimes it would be in the red-hot middle of the day when the only way to escape wishing to die was to keep working and perspiring, so that the oven-blast of the air would have something more than your hide to burn up. But usually it was in the dewy cool of the mornings, or in the evenings when the sun was not so full of sledge hammers—yes, usually it was when work was almost a pleasure that the press would give a groan, or a squeak, or a crack, and you could tell that something was sprained, or a bone broken somewhere.

Twice we had to spend half a day taking out the whole side of the box so as to work on the vitals of the affair. And again, something went wrong with the gears of the power beam, and we were a whole day out of pocket.

Yes, instead of averaging forty tons a day, we were averaging only about fifteen. It was sickening to think of!

But the only thing that kept us going and turning out even that much was the kid. He seemed to be able to read the mind of that machine, and he could tell in a moment just exactly what was wrong with it. He saved us time that way, and also he saved us a good deal by what he taught us about doing the work.

Before I was through, like the rest of the boys, I had tried my hand at everything on the job, from Jackson bucking to bale rolling and power driving. The bale rolling was the hardest and the most interesting.

All you had to do, when the driver yelled "Bale!" was to knock open the door with an iron bar, drop the bar, grab the five stiff wires as the wire-puncher shoved them through, cinch up and tie those wires with a fast figure eight—and if you were fast enough, you took the last wire right off the needle of the puncher—and then you hollered: "Tied!" And as the power driver started his team, the heater floated up, and as soon as it was clear of the table, the big first feed began to shoot down.

You had to get the bale out of the way and the door shut before that feed started to descend, and to do this meant grabbing the hay hook off the beam overhead, sinking it in the top edge of the bale, and while with one hand you jerked the bale out and broke it to the right across your knee, with the left hand you caught hold of the door, slammed it, and disengaging the hook from the bale you used that hook to pull over the locking bar.

After that, you simply had to roll the bale onto the scales, weigh it, write out its weight on a tag of redwood, and again on the page of your checking book, trundle the bale out to its place in the growing stack, and lift it into its berth, perhaps three feet high. Just as you were breaking your back to get that bale up, the power driver was sure to

43

yell "Bale!" again, and back you sprinted for the dog-house to do the whole thing over again.

Well, it was a pretty hot business, but it was a thing full of knacks from the tying of those infernal wires to the rolling and lifting of the bale itself. Little Chip knew all about the tricks. He could fair make the bales walk along the ground, and nobody in the outfit could punch the wires through fast enough to keep Chip from waiting for the last one to come.

Of course, he couldn't last long at it; but while he worked, he made things hum, and he showed us how to do it, and how to step so that not an inch was wasted. Sometimes it almost seemed as though he had built the first hay press in the world, he knew so much about the job!

But even the kid could not ward off the bad luck that followed that machine. And every day, what between the girl and the press, Newbold got blacker and blacker, and stared more and more at the ground, and not even Chip dared to sass him any longer.

Newbold used to walk out in the evening to the top of the nearest roll in the ground, and there he would stand as gaunt and melancholy as a scarecrow, staring over the surrounding acres, and weeping tears of blood in his heart because he knew that he would never have enough time, at this rate, to bale all the hay that he had cut. And to think of it lying there to first dry to powder, and then to be rotted by the winter rains, was enough to nearly kill him. He wasn't tight, I suppose; but it was a torture to him to see any wastage.

The atmosphere around that place grew more and more charged, and pretty soon all of us knew that it was only a question of time before the sparks would begin to jump—sparks that might burn the life out of some one!

The trouble was that, even if things had gone smoothly, we were cow-punchers, not mechanics. To do the same thing hour after hour was worse than a gun play on us!

That was about the time when Sheriff Murphy came out to visit us, and with his visit came the beginning of the end. It was just after dusk. We all lay around on our blankets, which we had rolled out on shocks of hay, the head end higher than the feet. Now we lay on our stomachs, our chins in our hands. Some of us smoked cigarettes. Some of the boys smoked pipes, but, for one reason or another, every few seconds there was a faint glow, and the face of some one stood out in rosy dimness at one part or other of the circle.

I remember that big Cash Logan was talking, at the time, and telling about how he once had a fight with a Canuck lumberman, a regular log-driver; and how the Canuck, being a little pressed, had pulled a knife to help out; and how he, Cash Logan, had used a trick he had learned when he was a boy, turning a handspring and whanging the soles of both shoes fairly and squarely into the face of the other fellow.

So he did that thing now, and the fellow he used as an example dropped with a groan, and half woke up and thought that he had been killed by a bullet through the brain, and then felt his sore and swelling face and roared out that he had been shot all full of holes.

"That's pretty good, Cash," said Pete Bramble, rubbing his sore face tenderly. "That's good enough to be written down, pretty near. Where did you read about it?"

"Read about it? Read about it?" yells Cash.

"That's what I said," remarked Bramble.

There might have been a fight on the spot, because neither of them were men likely to give ground on any subject, but just then we heard the jingle and the tramp of a horse coming up to the place, and then the sheriff's voice hailed us loudly.

He made quite a sensation.

For there were a number of the fellows working for the chief who preferred the misery of sticking to a job with him rather than the wretchedness of continually dodging the police.

Chapter Nine

It was an amusing but rather a nervous thing to see the way the boys of our outfit were shifting about a little, from side to side, and acting strained, and beginning to sift back away from the sheriff, picking themselves up from their shocks of hay, and going through all of the movements of dogs when they see a wolf in their midst.

Wise dogs, I mean, that have been wolf-stung once, and know enough to multiply every wolf by three or four when it comes to a fight. So these rough fellows, every one of whom, I suppose, had fallen foul of the law at some time or other, edged away from the sheriff.

The chief, however, started right up from his place and went to meet the man of the law. That was the good thing about Newbold. He always stood by and for his men in every pinch. They knew it. That was the chief reason that they kept in their hearts some kindness for him.

Now, as Newbold fronted up to the sheriff, the latter heaved himself down from his saddle with a grunt. His horse grunted, too, as though it was dead tired. And I remember how the reek of the mustang came sharply and clearly to my nostrils, and how, after a moment, I heard the steady dripping of the sweat that ran down from his belly to the ground.

The sheriff growled out a greeting of some sort to Newbold. Then he made and lighted a cigarette, and I had a good look at his face.

His name was Tug Murphy, and in those days he was quite a celebrity. The Tug stood for "tugboat," and the nickname was a fair one, because he was a fellow of broad beam and noisy ways, but a great deal of steady power always applied to the business of the county. I suppose he rode ten thousand miles a year, or even more than that. He galloped a good deal of crime out of that rough country, and a good deal of fear into the hearts of the crooks, so that every honest person in the district slept more soundly because of Tug Murphy, universal watchdog. He has finished his riding, now. One day he leaned into a cloud of dust that had a .45-caliber chunk in it, and the lead cut through Tug and carried away all of him except two hundred pounds of useless weight. Tug is forgotten now, but at the time of which I speak he had a name that worked miracles.

He was bow-legged and wide-shouldered. He had the look of a man always grinding his teeth and holding himself in. Anger seemed to be working up to a high head in him, day and night, and one waited to see him explode.

That was the look he had, red-faced, scowling, as he

46

lighted the cigarette. The flame fairly shone on his face, it was so running with perspiration.

He said in his rough, direct, brutal manner: "Hey, Newbold, why don't you feed your crew?"

"I feed my crew," said Newbold.

"You don't feed 'em enough to keep 'em from half starving," insisted the sheriff.

"Who told you that?" asked Newbold.

"They've been going over to the Seaton place lately, and slipping away with a few of the best chickens that they could lay their hands on," said the sheriff, "and old Seaton is a little tired of it. He didn't take the trouble to come over here and complain, but he took the trouble to come all the way to town, to tell me about it. Now, you look here, Newbold. You may not step over the traces yourself, but you're makin' trouble for others. And I ain't going to have it!"

Newbold said nothing. I thought that he was going to swallow these disagreeable remarks.

The sheriff, having made his first point, went on steadily:

"I'll tell you, Newbold, that they is some that approve of lynchin' hoss thieves. But my idea is that a man that would steal a hoss is a regular hero and a giant alongside of the poor, sneakin' skunk that goes and robs a henroost—"

Newbold said: "What you're doing is to call me a poor, sneakin' skunk, I think."

The sheriff answered: "You can put on the shoe, if it fits you."

"Peel off your coat and your badge," suggested Newbold, "and I'll see what your size is!"

"You wanta fight, do you?" said the sheriff. "And you think that I'll go around wasting my time fighting with fellows like you that don't mean anything to me? If I have to come and get you, Newbold, then I'll fight you, but I won't work over you for nothing."

I was surprised by this speech. I had thought that the sheriff really lived from day to day on the sweet prospect of the trouble he could find along the way. And here he was, nevertheless, avoiding a whole harvest field of it!

The rest of the boys picked up some spirit, when they heard the sheriff shutting down a little, as it were.

Pete Bramble said: "Nobody in this outfit is a chicken thief, sheriff. You've got this wrong."

"It wasn't a fox, and it wasn't a coyote, that got into the Seaton hen house and lifted chickens twelve nights running! A chicken every night. A fox or a coyote wouldn't work that way. It wasn't any of Seaton's own men, neither. He watched them for a week and they was always there; and the thievin' went on while the whole pack of them were under his eye. Now, where would the thief be likely to come from?"

"Out of the hills," said Pete Bramble. "Some Mexican who's lying up in the hills and don't want to waste ammunition for his meat."

"No," said the sheriff. "This ain't a Mexican."

"Why don't you give us a description of the crook?" said Newbold, with a sneer.

"I'll tell you a description of him," said the sheriff. "He's small enough to go through a window that a full-sized man couldn't wriggle his stomach through. And he's quick enough to catch a chicken and dodge the load of a shotgun that he's touched off with his own hand. That handful of buckshot, it ought to have blown him in two, but the crook dodged fast enough to get away, it seems, and there was no blood on his back trail. He's a small, fast, tricky feller. He's probably got a face like a fox, because that's what he is—a regular fox on two legs. Old Seaton has taken three shots at him, and never had no luck, and set a dozen different kind of traps, and still he keeps right on stealin'. He's a mean, hardy feller. And you've got a whole pack of mean, hardy fellers here, Newbold."

I was a good deal interested by this account of the persistent chicken thief; and, to be sure, the fare in our cook house was enough to drive any man to drink—or chicken stealing!

"You figger that I've starved out my boys," said Newbold, "and when they passed the plate the second time, I've poured hot water into it. That's the way that you've figgered. And then they got hold of an inspired chicken thief and they sent him out and he raided the coop every night, eh? But I'll tell you what, sheriff. You're barking up the wrong tree altogether."

"I'm gunna have a look, just the same," said the sheriff.

"Take your look, and be danged, then," said the boss. "But if this outfit started to stealing chickens, they wouldn't stop with one a night. Lemme tell you something, sheriff. The kind of men that I keep out here, there's nothing but real men among 'em. The kind of men that I've got around here, they would eat a chicken each just to sort of get their appetites limbered up. If they got going on the Seaton chickens, they'd carry off half a dozen apiece; and when they got through crunching up the chickens, they'd eat the Seatons, bones and all. You can tell Pa Seaton that, from me, and tell Ned and Harry Seaton, too. I've gotta mind to saddle and ride right now over to see the Seatons! Chicken thieves, eh? That's the kind of men I hire, is it? Chicken thieves!"

He was furious.

Said the sheriff: "You cool yourself off a little, will you? The fact is that I've made up my mind to it. One of your men has been doin' it!"

"That would mean," suggested Newbold, "a trip of about five miles each way. And I tell you what, after my boys have finished wrestling with this here hay press all the day long, there's dang little energy left in 'em. They don't even cuss at the cook any more. Speakin' personal, I'd rather be sentenced to a prison for sixteen years than to a darned hay press for sixteen days!"

And he snorted like a horse, as he spoke, and from his circle of men there came a deep-throated murmur of sympathetic understanding.

"Let's get down to business," suggested the sheriff.

"That's what I've been standing here waiting for," answered Newbold.

"How many men you got out here with you?"

"Seven."

"That doesn't count you?"

"No."

"Does it count the cook?"

"Yes."

"Lemme see them seven line up," said the sheriff.

"You line 'em up yourself," said the chief, more and more angry. "You can see the cook over there in the cook house working at his stove. I wish he'd cook himself, dang him! And here's the rest of the boys."

"There's five here," said the sheriff.

I counted the same number, including myself.

"Oh, that leaves the kid out," said the chief. "And he's turned in and gone to sleep."

"What kid?" said the sheriff. "Where does he sleep?"

"Right yonder. You can see his hat, there. He sleeps with his hat on. He's a tough kid for you!"

"Lemme have a look at him," said the sheriff. "Hey, kid!"

"Leave him be," suggested the chief. "He's tired. He does the work of two men all day long."

"And gets the pay for half a man, I suppose," suggested the other. "Hey, kid, stand up and lemme look at you."

Chip did not stir. The sheriff walked over to him, and I grinned to myself, thinking of the fine flow of language with which the boy would certainly drench down the sheriff, when the officer arrived.

The sheriff leaned. Then he straightened up, holding Chip at arm's length, dangling.

Not Chip, after all, but only Chip's hat, and his blanket attached to his hat, and out of the blanket streamed down the hay which the kid had twisted up inside, so as to give the effect of being a boy asleep there.

The sheriff let the stuff drop. It collapsed on the ground as he turned to Newbold.

"Your men ain't chicken thieves, eh?" said he. "Then your boys are!"

Chapter Ten

I saw Newbold turn a little to one side and then to another.

"Leave the boy be," said he. "You've got nothing on him."

"Not yet," said the sheriff, "but I'm going to have!"

"He's right around here," said Newbold miserably. "He's sure to be right around here. He was here just a minute ago. I saw him."

"You don't see him now," answered the sheriff, "and you won't see him later on, either, until he's got some extra filling inside of his stomach, I guess. Oh, he's a bright lad, all right!"

"You're wrong," said Newbold. "The kid's the best kid that I ever saw."

A sort of a rumbling chorus came from all of us. He was the best kid. He was also the meanest, most cantankerous, sassiest, most trouble-brewing kid.

Steal chickens?

He would as soon steal chickens as play marbles or go shooting. The minute the idea was suggested, we could all feel that stealing chickens would be worth a five-mile ride to the boy. Simple enough, too. He would merely catch up one of the horses that was wandering around near the house and he would jog away, and the rest of us would be asleep in two shakes after we had turned in.

It would take a man made of steel to work all day the way Chip worked and then go off for half the night. But boys can do what men never could do. If they begin to run down, they can wind themselves up and go right on ticking again.

"All right," said the sheriff. "I've found out what I want to know. Of course, he's a good kid. He'd have to be good to steal chickens so well. So long, boys."

He mounted his horse again and started off at a jog, lining out across country in the direction of the Seaton place.

"That's the dickens!" said the chief, and began to swear.

"We ought to send somebody out to cut in ahead of the sheriff and warn the kid," said Pete Bramble.

"The kid would never let you get up close enough to give him a warning," said Newbold. "He rides like a dang jockey."

That was a fact. We wouldn't be likely to get up close to the boy.

But, at any rate, I felt that I couldn't stay away from the trouble. I was nervous, and I just wanted to be on hand to see what was what. So I saddled up a horse and left the rest of them discussing what a mean chap the sheriff was, and cut across country on his line.

51

I hadn't gone very far when I saw the loom of him before me.

He turned around, pulled up his horse, and waited for me with a gun in his hand.

"It's all right," I sang out to him. "I'm just your posse, sheriff. I've come up from Newbold's camp to help you out."

"A lot of help anybody from Newbold's camp will be to me!" grunted Tug. "But come along, if you want to. I wish that we could get close enough to see the little rat doing his tricks in that hen house! It's a caution!"

A trace of enthusiasm came into his voice.

"Seaton has been pretty worried," I suggested.

The sheriff actually laughed.

"Seaton's an old-timer, a trapper," he said. "He thinks that he knows how to catch everything that walks and breathes. Well, he can't catch this kid. Maybe we can't. It's going to be a hunt and a chase. That's what it is!"

He laughed again.

I never had dreamed that Tug Murphy could show such a trace of good humor as he was showing now. It was a surprise. A thing not to be dreamed of. I played him along on this line. I told him that the boy was wild and tough, but the gamest that ever stepped, and the best sport, and the rightest kind of a lad.

He listened to me and seemed to believe that what I said might have some truth in it

We rode along at a good clip. Then the sheriff admitted to me that he was a little worried.

"I never had to play against a kid before," he said. "Yes, against what we call kids—boys of nineteen or so that are as strong as a man and as fast with a gun, and sometimes a good deal straighter in their shooting. I've had those lads to handle, and some tough times they've given me. But suppose I take into jail a brat of fifteen or so— Well, how old is this Chip?"

"Fifteen," said I.

He let out a small-sized shout.

"Fifteen!" said he. "And Seaton has dragged me out here on this rotten business? I'll tell him what I think of him."

"You tell him that Newbold is going to call on him, too," said I, grinning in the dark.

52

"He wanted to fight me, that Newbold," said the sheriff, and chuckled again. "He's all right. Anybody's all right—anybody that's always ready to fight when he's dead sober! You bet he's all right. Newbold is all right!"

I thought that Tug Murphy, for that matter, was all right, too. He was climbing up in my estimation all the time. I never had talked with any one exactly like him, and the more he said, the more I wanted to hear.

I told him that he was dead right about Newbold.

"Sure I'm right," said the sheriff. "He wanted to fight me because of the kid. What's the kid to him? Nothing! No kin! But he wanted to fight me because of the kid. Anybody's all right that will fight for kids that don't belong to them."

I agreed again. The sheriff kept chuckling.

"Here I've gone and used up one of my best nags," he said. "Look at that! All on account of a dang kid."

And he laughed aloud once more. He had a strange sense of humor, which this case appealed to.

"I'll bet the kid is Irish," he said.

"He has the reddest hair you ever saw," said I.

"Sure he's Irish," said Tug Murphy. "I knew it right off. Something told me. He's all right, too. The kid is all right. He's stealing those chickens every night. That's what makes him all right."

I did not understand this. I failed so completely to understand that I admitted I did not follow his line of thought.

He explained to me: "Well, you look at here. If he stole just for stealing, he would've cleaned out the chicken house the first trip, wouldn't he?"

I admitted that he would.

"And if he stole because he was just hungry, he'd quit as soon as he found out there were dogs watching for him, and men, and rifles, and shotgun traps all set to blow the tar out of him. He'd quit when he found out those things, wouldn't he? You certainly can't digest very good when you've got a hole blowed clean through your stomach, can you?"

"No," I admitted. "You couldn't do that."

"You see how it is," went on the sheriff, getting more and more enthusiastic. "He kept going back because there was the shotgun traps and everything and every-

53

body all set to catch him. That's why he went back. It was a game. He liked it. He even liked having the dogs run him."

"Have the dogs run him?" I asked.

"Sure they have! And he threw them off the trail. Right when they had a clear view of him. The dogs had, I mean, and they started to run with their heads up. But he chucked them. He got among some rocks and he chucked them. And he goes back every night and plays the game again. Because he's Irish, see? That's the way an Irishman would do. I knew he was Irish right off."

He continued to chuckle and to be very pleased. It gradually dawned on me that Tug Murphy was Irish himself.

"You take a kid like that," went on the sheriff, "if he don't get hanged, he grows up and makes a real man. That's the kind of men that you need to have. The real ones. They raise a little trouble, but when they settle down, there's something to them."

"There's something to the kid," I agreed very heartily.

"How often have you missed him away at night?" asked the sheriff.

"Never have missed him at all, till tonight," I said.

"Not till an Irishman came there and showed you he was gone," chuckled Tug Murphy. "It takes a thief—"

He stopped himself short, and hurried on, rather embarrassed: "He's Irish. He's smart, you never missed him away. Not for more'n two weeks, and he's been gone every night. He's a fox. He's smart. You never would've guessed, except that I came out there and gave you a lead."

Now, as we went along at a good gallop through the hills, we saw the loom of something far before us, going over a hill and disappearing into the sky line among the stars.

"That's the kid," said the sheriff. "He's going slow. He's traveling dead easy. That's a mistake. But the best of 'em get overconfident at times. And he don't know that an Irishman is after him. He don't have any idea of that. But maybe he's going slow so's he can be thinking out the way he'll turn the trick tonight."

I agreed that that really might be the idea.

We continued to gain on the rider before us, and

presently we were so close that we could clearly distinguish that the rider was very small.

"No saddle," said the sheriff, who had amazingly good eyes at night. "You see how it is with him? He don't take no saddle along, because he don't want to leave no easy signs behind him. You take a saddle, the blanket of it would still be wet in the morning and give him away. He goes bareback. Yeah, he's Irish, all right."

He still continued to chuckle. He seemed the most contented man in the world. But now he reined in his horse a little.

"There's no use crowding the kid too much," said he. "We might as well see how he does the trick, if we can. I'll pay for the chicken he catches."

"Maybe he'll only catch a load of buckshot," I suggested.

"You can't shoot an Irishman with buckshot," he declared. "It takes a slug out of a Colt or a rifle to stop an Irishman. No, the boy will come through, all right. He'll get the chicken again. A fellow like that Seaton, he never could catch an Irish kid like Chip. He has red hair, didn't you say? I sort of guessed that he had red hair, like that."

It seemed that there was to be no argument between us about the qualities and the importance of Chip. And now we came up through the hills to the gap from which we could look out and down toward the house of Seaton.

Chapter Eleven

The boy was not there.

At least, the silhouette of the small rider no longer appeared, and, instead, we had only the dim sweep of the hollow, with two higher hills beyond, square-topped, like two raised fists. In the midst of the hollow, two lights shone from the Seaton ranch house. We made out the shoulders and the roof line of it by degrees, and then the staggered lines of corral fencing, the outhouses, and a lantern walking across the picture toward the house.

"We'd better ride straight in, if we're to warn Seaton," I suggested.

The officer of the law only grunted.

"Seaton be danged!" he said. "Let Seaton take his chance! We're too late and too far behind to watch the kid at his work. We'd only scare him away. And it's a lot better if we just cut him off when he tries to retreat. We'll catch him with the goods on him. That'll teach him a lesson. That'll learn him to be a decent boy and man—"

The sheriff began his laughter once more.

He dismounted; he lighted a cigarette; he whistled, and he hummed to himself.

I got down in turn. It was hot, there in the gap. The rocks on either hand were still throwing off the heat which the sun had poured thickly over them during the day. There was a sticky smell, like new varnish in a closed house, that came from the weeds that grew about us, and now and then there was a small rustling from the clumps of shrubbery which gave a false promise of a wind that never came.

The walking lantern reached the house and passed inside. A moment later, we heard the far-away sound of the jingling slam of the screen door.

"Now, the last man's back into the ranch house," said the sheriff. "The last man's back inside, and the trap's all set for the kid, and the dogs, and the guns, and the hunters, are all ready. And here we are, to cut off his retreat. And all on account of one red-headed brat of an Irish kid! That's the kind of men they breed, the Irish! They've got more glory and stretched more rope than any two other nations. That's the kind they are."

I could not help saying: "This sounds to me like a queer sort of law enforcement, sheriff. But you're the boss. Only one thing I'm really bothered about— Suppose that trap closes on the kid and breaks his back! There'll be some pretty angry men back there with the hay press, beginning with the boss."

"Shut up!" said the sheriff. "What do you think I'm worried about, myself? But he's gotta pull through and I—"

Just then, in the middle of his words, as a wave breaks over a rock at the entrance and floods all over a cave with roaring, and dashings, and echoes, just so out of the hollow there broke a clamor that had in it guns exploding, men shouting, dogs yelling and howling, and even the neighing of horses.

"There they go!" yipped the sheriff.

"Poor Chip!" I said to myself, and hardly dared to think of what might have happened.

That uproar might have been the blasting away of a mountainside, or a half regiment of soldiers!

It did not die down, all at once, but stretched out into a point, as it were, running in a long arm from the ranch house, and straight toward us!

"He's gone away!" I shouted.

"I told you he would!" answered the sheriff.

And he struck me between the shoulder blades and bruised me to the heart.

"They can't catch the tricky little rabbit!" I said, and smote the sheriff's shoulder, and felt it sag beneath the stroke.

"Not in ten million years!" said the sheriff. "Not now that he's begun to run. But look! Look!"

We could see them very clearly. It looked as though a dozen riders were galloping out from the house, the starlight fingering very faintly the sweating horses. In the dust of their raising, a fog closed over the house, and only its lights glittered through. But what made my heart stand still was the yelling of the dogs.

"They've got hounds there that'll chew man-meat as easy as venison," I suggested to the sheriff.

"They've got Butch Wafer's pack," said the sheriff. "But they won't find that brat! He'll—he'll fade right out away from under their noses!"

However, the sheriff was not as confident as his words: There was a tremor in his voice, and a hesitation in his speech.

I strained my eyes into the darkness; I could see the hunted swerving a little from this side to that; and then a new note came into the chanting of the hounds.

"They've got him under their teeth!" I told the sheriff. "You and your fool ideas—those man-eaters are right onto his heels—and they're running in full view! That's what

57

they're doing! You and your ideas—both are not worth a cent!"

The sheriff gripped me by the arm.

"If I thought—" he began. "Come on, son. We'll run our horses down there and take a chance at them. We'll stop them. If they've so much as touched the hide of the brat, I'll—"

He stopped. There was a good reason. For the dogs no longer yelled so confidently. The sound of their voices split apart and traveled to both sides.

"They've lost again!" declared the sheriff, instantly confident. "They've lost again, and the kid has won."

"You're Irish, too," said I. "Wait a minute! But the dogs sure seemed to lose that trail—but then—they were plumb running on his heels, to hear the yap of 'em, and I've heard that pack singing before!"

"Aw, they're beat! They're beat!" said the sheriff.

We could hear the hunters shouting and cursing, and casting the hounds ahead, now here, now there.

Presently the hounds strung out in a long line on a scent which one of them had picked up. The men whooped them on. Out of the dust of their own raising we saw that hunt streaming through the night. Still, I could not feel that there was any real confidence in the voice of the pack. It had not the ring that keeps dwelling in the backbone of the strongest man.

Then the roar struck a hollow in the hills beside us, and turned at once to a remote music, and floated upward, and away.

"They'll never get the kid tonight," I could not help saying.

"You've been talking like a fool," the sheriff gasped, with a long, long breath. "This is the first sensible thing you've said. What've I been tellin' you all the time about—"

He stopped clicking his teeth together with surprise.

For a small whistle wavered up from the dark of the hollow before us, and it was answered by a whinny from among the rocks near by.

A small whistle, and a small nicker of a horse, mind you! And then the sheriff began to curse softly beneath his breath. I was swearing, too. From not ten yards away

58

from us, a mustang trotted out of a patch of shrubbery. Not ten yards away from us, mind you!

And down it went into the hollow, and there we made out faintly the small form of the boy.

We saw him meet the horse. We saw him carrying something in his hand. We saw him slick onto the back of the horse and go jogging away at a slant from the place where we waited.

He began to laugh; and it seemed to me that that laughter was the blood-brother to the sound of the sheriff's mirth that I had listened to so much during this dark ride. The very same, but a little thinner, and farther away.

"Now we climb after him!" said the sheriff to me.

That was what we did. We rode out of the gap, and swinging to the left, we just kept the loom of the rider within our eyes.

He took an odd course, considering that he was due back to the hay-press camp before so very long. I mean, our sleeping hours were always too short for me, and if the kid insisted on having his fun every evening after dark, one would think that, once the game was played, he'd strike out in a bee line for the camp.

But he didn't travel as a bird flies. He was rounding away off to the right of the line, and heading under a junk heap of naked hills so bare and polished by the palming of the wind that the rocks gleamed even under the stars.

Under the side of these rocks, the boy dismounted, and leaving the mustang behind him, he disappeared among the big stones.

The sheriff was worried, and shook his head.

"Why should he do that?" he asked. "Why should he ride away over here to this spot to cook his chicken?"

Inspiration struck me dumb, all in a moment.

"There's somebody inside those rocks waiting for him, Tug!" said I.

He grunted.

"Maybe so," said he. "Maybe there is a brain or two can be rounded up inside of that head of yours."

We left our horses near the mustang from which Chip had dismounted, and cut in at the spot where he had entered. We went as softly, you can be sure, as though we were walking up on the camp fire of a batch of red Indians.

For what might it not be that the boy was heading toward in there in the rocks?

Well, we had the glint, and then the gleam of fire before us, after a few moments; and after that, the stir of voices to help us along.

We had taken a good many minutes to follow the trail, but we arrived in time, after all. For when we came up through the rocks to a point where we could lie low and see the flicker and waning of the fire, and then the big leap of the blaze when the breeze touched it—when we came to this point, I say, and stretched out to see what we could see, we were just in time to catch the kid come out of the dark gap between two rocks, and with him, leaning an arm across his shoulders and looming mighty pale and thin, there was a grown man.

That was why the lad stole food every night!

But the way that Chip supported that tall, lank form was the strangest thing to see; even his voice had changed and turned tender.

"I heard a lot of racket down there," the man was saying. "I thought that they were after me again!"

"Naw," said the boy. "They haven't got the brains to hunt up here for you. I told you that you'd be safe here, Mr. Waters!"

Hai! How the sound of that name jumped through me! For there was White Water, and the kid beside him, and the sheriff lying ready in the dark to take them both!

Chapter Twelve

It was White Water, well enough, but a good deal faded since I last saw him.

He was thinner, leaner, lankier. And he was so weak that Chip had to steady him a little as he sat down near the fire. Still, there was the old grip about his jaws, and the look in his eyes.

"It's better out here, ain't it?" asked Chip.

Waters sighed. He stretched his arms and then let his head fall back against the rock that was behind him.

"Better? It's worlds better!" said he. "By Heaven, son, the shake and the flare of that little fire warms up the soul of me. And then to have the sight of the stars is worth more than I can tell you."

"Yeah," said the boy. "I bet there was days when you never thought that you'd have a look at those stars again."

"Yeah, there was days like that, all right," said the outlaw. "You know how it is, son. Lying there flat, with the fever in me, and the strength out—that was sort of tough."

The boy was sitting down cross-legged, and was busily pulling away the feathers of the chicken. He stopped his work for a moment, and he looked at the crook.

"Jiminy, Mr. Waters," said he, "I bet it was bad! And the water that I set in there beside you, I bet it got pretty warm during the end of the day, didn't it?"

"It got a little soupy," said Waters.

He turned his head and smiled at the boy, and there was love in his eyes.

Well, he had reason to love Chip.

"But the nights," said Waters. "They were the times when I would have given up, and let go all holds, and then I would have sunk into water as dark as any ocean, Chip, and just a little deeper than the sea."

"Ay," said the boy, "I disremember when it was that I woke up kind of sick and dizzy in the middle of one night, and I was sort of choking with a bad dream. And all at once, I remembered that I was alone in the house, and that there was nobody to bring a hand to me—I was pretty sick, I'll tell you."

He stripped the chicken white and clean beneath its feathers and began to cut it up. He was a regular little butcher. I never saw neater work done.

"But when those bad times came, Chip," said the outlaw, "I could always remember that you had been there to see me; and that you'd surely come the next night, too; and that some way or other, I ought to fight it out—after all the work you'd put in on me."

"Hey! It's been no work," said Chip. "It's been fun."

He chuckled as he said it. His eyes danced as he looked at the other.

"Yeah," said Waters. "You seem to like it, all right. Don't your uncle get tired of losing a chicken a night?"

"He hasn't noticed yet," said that little liar. "He's gotta lot of chickens. He's got near thousands of 'em, pretty near."

"I'll pay him double for every one, Chip," said Waters earnestly.

"Aw, sure you will," answered Chip. "You don't have to worry about that. It don't make no real difference."

"No real difference," said Waters. "Only life or death, to me. But I've wondered if you haven't been in danger, Chip, stealing this meat and getting it out to me."

"Danger?" said Chip, yawning a little. "What sort of danger would there be in picking up a chicken? Or ten chickens at a time? You know the way that it is on a big old ranch. You know how! Aw, they roost everywhere. On a fence, or on the shoulder of a stack, or on the woodpile under the roof of the woodshed. All you gotta do is to walk along and put out a hand, on that farm of my uncle's, and you're sure to run into a chicken before very long."

"I imagine that you have a guiding instinct, son, as the preachers say," remarked Waters.

"Maybe," grinned the boy.

He was cutting up the chicken and putting it on small, sharpened sticks. He gave two of these to the outlaw, and he took two himself. They began to turn the spits, and the smell of that good, roasting meat made my mouth water, after the fare we'd been having at the cook house.

"Tell me something, Chip," said Waters. "There were a few days, back there, when you only pretended to think I was better. You really thought that I was worse!"

Chip sat up straight, with a jerk and a start.

"I'll tell you, Mr. Waters, tonight," said he. "There was never a time when I was sure that you were going to pull through. Never a time, I mean, until tonight! You always looked kind of slipping, night after night. It used to make me sick, to look at you. Aw, you were mighty sick, Mr. Waters!"

"Stop calling me that," said the other. "Call me Joe, or Bill, or Ed, or Nick, or anything, It doesn't matter."

The boy was lost in thought, slowly turning the roasting meat, while the fumes of the cooking arose from it.

"I might call you 'Chief,'" he suggested. "I couldn't call you nothing small. You know that I was there when the three of them cornered you, and the three went down, and you got out. After that, I couldn't call you nothing small."

"Because I'm a thug and know how to fight with guns," said Waters, rather sadly, "you look up to me a little. Well, I—"

"It ain't that," insisted the boy. "It's just because when the pinch comes, you don't lie down. Look at anybody else, with three slugs through him, he would've gone in and given himself up."

"And be hanged, Chip?" suggested the outlaw.

"Yeah," drawled the boy, still thinking fiercely. "Hanging ain't so bad, either. First, they get out a lot of newspaper writing. And then everybody talks of the trial. And then there's a female league of something or other's daughters, or something like that, that comes along and gets up a petition for a pardon. And the governor gets gray-headed saying 'no'; and somebody writes a book about you; and then there's a lot of fun before the end, and maybe it's only life imprisonment; and then the boss of the prison, he makes you his confidential secretary and guard, and you don't do nothing but sit in leather chairs, and hang your heels on the edge of a desk, and smoke fat cigars, and write your reminiscences, and everybody looks up to you a lot and says there goes the guy that killed eleven men—or how many men have you really killed, Chief?"

"Four," said the outlaw, "and Heaven help me for doing it. Where did you pick up all this about prisons and such?"

"You know," said the boy. "You can't help readin' the interestin' part of the newspaper and listenin' to the interestin' talk in the bunk houses. You see me, Chief? Well, when I grow up, I'm gunna be free, too."

"Free?" asked the outlaw.

"Yeah. You know."

"No, I don't know. What do you mean by 'being free'?"

"I mean—puttin' up your own hoss into somebody else's barn. That's what I call bein' free."

Waters smiled, but his smile was wan.

The chicken was now ready for eating, but before Waters began on it, he said:

"I'll tell you the truth, old son. Being free means chilblains in winter and sun-scalding in summer; and one meal or none a day; and the life of a wolf; and no friend you can trust; and no home, no wife, no children. Or if you have 'em, they're raised by somebody else. Being free means living on the outside of about everything that's worth while."

"Except freedom?" questioned Chip.

"Yes," said Waters slowly. "Except that, perhaps. Here you, Chip. You take my advice. I know about that stuff. You go and get it out of your mind. That's the only way to do."

"I'm gunna watch and make up my own mind," said Chip. "Look at me. I wouldn't be your friend, Chief, if it wasn't that I had seen you livin' free. Everybody looks up to free things. Who minds a tame duck more'n a pig in the mud? But a wild duck looks pretty fine, and the wild geese honking south or north, they give you the prickles up your backbone, and you want to break away. You know that's true."

"That's true," said Waters. Then he changed the subject. "You've gotta eat part of this chicken tonight, son," said he, quickly.

"Me?" said the boy, with an air of surprise. "Sure, I ain't gonna eat any of it. I'm full."

I thought of the sort of food and portions that Chip enjoyed along with the rest of us in the cook house, and smiled a little.

"When I was your age, I was never full," said the outlaw.

"You know how it is around a farm," said Chip. "You know there's always something lying around to eat. And if you get a pang, you can go and snitch something out of the pantry."

"Whatcha have for supper tonight?" asked the other.

"Me? Oh, we had venison steaks. They'd been hung a little too long, but I'm used to 'em that way; and they was prime and tender. And we had hominy, and corn bread with heaps of butter onto it, and ras'berry jam, and bread pudding full of raisins, and mashed potatoes, and baked sweet potatoes, too, and string beans, and pork

64

chops for them that didn't want the venison. So I had some of both. Outside of that we didn't have nothing much but some hard candy, and coffee and cream, and doughnuts. My aunt, she makes the primest doughnuts that you ever seen. That's about all I had to eat, but what made you ask?"

I thought of the cook-house dinner, and grinned again.

Waters was looking hard at the boy, and I could see that he was thoroughly doubting what he had heard, but he said nothing, for a moment.

At last he remarked: "Chip, your job is getting me on my feet, and you're doing it mighty well. I've got no right to question you about how and where you manage all this, but I reckon that your back trail would be pretty hard to follow and pretty interesting, too. Well, here's my regards!"

And, with that, he started in on a quarter of chicken and began to reduce it to a white bone.

"You're looking a lot better," said the boy. "You'll be fit to ride, pretty quick."

"I could ride right now," said the outlaw. "Only I'd like to wait a while till there's a litte grip and strength in my knees. You know how it is, Chip."

"You bet I know. You'd be crazy to try to ride now," said Chip.

"I guess he'll try, though," said the sheriff, and stepped into the firelight with a pair of guns.

Chapter Thirteen

It staggered me.

There was something in that scene between the boy and the outlaw that had prevented me from even thinking about the sheriff's presence. But there he stood, with his two guns looking as large and a lot more deadly than cannons.

The boy got up and reached for a stone. Waters simply stretched across and knocked the stone out of his hand.

"When a game's finished," he said, gravely, "there's only one thing for it, and that's to give up your chair. I'll qualify, now, for all that newspaper publicity that you were talking about, Chip!"

He was dead game, was poor Waters. He could smile as he said it.

I thought that Chip had colic, he was so bent and twisted with rage and pain, but the sheriff unquestionably had the upper hand.

I said to him:

"Look here, Tug. The fact is that you could give a man a chance when—"

The sheriff favored me with a glint out of one eye.

"Give a low hound a second chance?" he roared. "Give a low, sneakin' hound a second chance?" A gent that goes out and lets a poor kid risk his neck every night to bring him food? He ain't a man. If he was half a man, I'd let him. I'd give him my own hoss to start him on the way, just because Chip, the crooked little chicken thief, thinks so much of him. But he ain't a man. I'd like to grind him under my heel to show him what I think of him. That's what I'd like to do."

Now, that ended the argument on the spot, as far as I was concerned. Because I saw that the Irish was up in Tug, and when the rage is in the head of an Irishman, there's no making him see reason, or kindness, or humor.

Then the kid came up and gave me a nudge.

"You could make a play, Joe!" he said. "Now you got your chance. You just trip up Tug from behind, and me and the Chief will do the rest!"

Yes, he would have tackled the sheriff, single-handed. That was the Irish in him!

But poor Waters went off to jail, holding himself erect in the saddle, for the benefit of Chip; but I could see by the tremor in his shoulders how weak he was.

Chip stood beside him, and watched the two ride off. And as he watched them, he talked in a way that curdled my blood to hear. For a boy should not know all the words and the ideas that Chip was master of, and the description he gave of the sheriff's probable end was brilliant and entirely too incandescent.

Well, we stood and watched them go out of sight, and

then we went back toward the camp, and got to the hay press in a dead silence.

There was only one speech from the boy, and that was when we were about to turn in.

"How much would a dog-gone good lawyer want to defend a man?" he asked. "Would he want as much as thirty dollars?"

That, you see, was about what Chip must have saved from his wages!

It gave me a lump in the throat. I told him that I thought thirty would be plenty, and if it wasn't I'd help him out, and so would some of the other boys.

"No," said Chip, as he slid into his blankets. "He wouldn't like it. The Chief wouldn't, I mean—if the hat was passed for him."

So I fell asleep, and they had to fairly drag me out of my blankets when the dawn broke on the next wretched day. I looked about me for Chip, but Chip was nowhere to be seen. And he didn't turn up later. He was gone, and I knew where. He was gone to find, hire, or beg a lawyer to defend his hero.

Poor Chip!

I forgot all about Waters, though, before the day was very old. So did all of us. I told the boys at breakfast the story of the night before, and what they said about the sheriff was not a pleasant thing to hear.

Only the boss sat still, leaning over his coffee cup and stirring in the so-called sugar, and no doubt snarling silently, but never saying a word. I thought that he looked pleased, rather than otherwise.

But he forgot about Waters. So did I. So did all the rest as the day wore along, and we not only saw but felt that the kid was no longer among us!

I say that we felt it, because everything went wrong from the start.

When the wires were used up, the cook was brought out and started in twisting and cutting at the machine which the kid had made to hum. But it didn't hum now. Those wires came off one at a time, lamely. And there was a flow of music from that wire-cutting machine that darkened the sky and yet made the day a lot hotter.

Finally, the cook came over to the dog-house, where the boss was tying a bale, and that cook stood up on the weighing machine and made a speech that was worth listening to; and he said that the cook house had been a lot worse than misery to him from the start; and that he hoped he'd made us suffer some; and that he wished he'd made us suffer more; and that of all the lot of greasy hobos he ever had seen we were the worst, and that the boss was the cheapest of the lot; and he hoped that we'd all go to blazes and each of us be stationed at a wire-cutting machine, but that for his part, he was through with the outfit, then and there!

In fact, he quit on the spot, with the boss's hay hook sailing after him and whizzing past his ear.

We were all sorry to see that hay hook miss its mark.

Then I was dragged off the feeding table and put at the wire cutter. Well, a wire cutter is not such a complicated machine, but this one was mean. It was second-hand, like all the rest of the outfit, and it was loose in its joints, and could not be tightened. It was sprained here, and had rheumatism there, and how the kid had made it jump so fast was a mystery to me. I couldn't turn out wires of the same length and the same strength. Either they were stretched so much that they broke where the beater rose and let the bale stretch, or else they were so slack that they twisted like long, thin, black snakes.

But worst of all, I couldn't make the cutting lever work well, and there were twists and turns on nearly every wire end. The wire puncher almost went mad over them; and the chief cursed me with every bale that he rolled to the pile.

It was a bad day.

By the time it came for the morning lunch, I was getting so many black looks that I went off by myself and ate my prunes and hard tack and swallowed my coffee and didn't have the courage to go back for a second cup.

The wire puncher was given the job as cook on the understanding that the first man to complain would have to take his place. He said that he guaranteed complaints, too!

It was a pretty black morning, and the lunch that waited for us at the end of it did not help our humor along, very much.

Just to cap everything, along came the girl.

I mean, Marian Wray came riding up, and first off we

68

were glad to see her; but the first thing that she asked for was Chip. And while we were waiting to find an answer, she went on to say that he was the finest boy in the world, and that her father was riding over specially to see him and try to persuade him to take up a civilized existence.

Then everybody looked at me, so I had to come out with the story of what had happened the night before. I knew that it was going to be bad, but none of us guessed how bad it would be.

When I had finished, she said coldly:

"And you stood there, and let one man, one brutal so-called officer of the law, take away that poor, sick fellow?"

I stammered. I didn't find any words. I felt pretty sick, and must have looked sicker.

She saw that she had sunk me with all on board, and she turned and gave her heavier guns to Newbold. Her smile was a thing of beauty.

"But if Chip has gone off to save his friend," said she, "I know that you're going to help him, and nothing can stop you!"

Newbold stood up and pointed to the hay press. A wind was puffing at it, and knocking off the chaff and the dust, so that it seemed to be smoking.

"If there was a silver-trimmed angel came down from heaven, Marian," says he, "and blew his trumpet in my ear, I wouldn't leave this here job until I'd finished it! That's a fact!"

She only shook her head.

"Ah," says she, "I know the real tenderness of heart under the hard exteriors of men like you! You know perfectly well that poor little Chip—the darling!—will be trying to break into that jail to get his hero out—and he'll land in the reform school trying to do it. But I know you won't let it come to that! I simply know!"

She gave Newbold a shining look. His face pinched as though he had been hit on the chin. He took two strides that brought him away from us and right up to her. He was as dusty as the hay press. The shoulders of his flannel shirt were white with dried, caked perspiration.

"Marian," he said, "don't talk to me like that. What's

that fellow Waters to me—or to you? You know where I stand. But what's Waters to me, I ask you?"

He was serious. The rest of us looked down at our hands. We saw that Newbold was pleading with her, and it was a funny thing to hear Newbold pleading.

"What do I care about Waters?" says the girl, quick as a flash. "Not a snap of the fingers—except that he's sick. Not a breath—except that poor little Chip loves him. And I trust a man that such a boy loves. But I know that you'll change your mind and do something about it. I've thought that you're the biggest sort of man that I ever laid eyes on, and I know that I'm not wrong. I can't be wrong!"

Newbold pointed at her a finger like a leveled gun.

"You want me to go and leave this job and pry a thug out of jail?" says he, quietly.

"Ex-act-ly!" says she, as precise as a school-teacher.

"This is my job!" says Newbold. "And I won't quit it. Not for Waters. Not for the kid." He had worked himself up to the climax. "Not for you" he wound up.

She made a step back from him.

"Now I understand," said she, nodding at him. "I ought to thank you. You let me see you for the first time. I thought there was something grand and heroic about you. I see that you're only—a farm hand!"

Chapter Fourteen

I had a big brother once. I spent most of my time hating him, because he was bigger and stronger than I, and he could tease me until I was frantic, and there was nothing that I could do about it. I used to pray that something would happen to him, and one day it came about so. He was having a fight with a smaller boy than himself, after school, in the vacant lot. That smaller boy was a newcomer. He was freckled, and had dusty-colored hair, and his eyes were a little crooked, and he grinned and was white about the mouth as he fought.

But he knew how to box. He was knocked down three

times; but he kept coming up, and finally he learned how to duck under my brother's arms, and gave him a fair pasting. He blacked my brother's eyes for him, and cut his mouth, and punched him in the stomach till he groaned, and on the jaw till he whined.

And at first I liked it, but afterward I began to grow sick, and sicker. And finally I prayed for the skies to drop on all of us, just to end that picture of my brother's shame.

And that was the way I felt, for one, when I stood by and saw Newbold take his licking from that girl.

She simply got into the saddle and rode off again. But Newbold stood still, as though he had dropped anchor in a harbor of thought.

Poor Newbold!

He had bullied and beaten us all, at his pleasure, but still it was a horrible thing to see a fellow like him so hurt by the unjustifiable words of a mere slip of a girl. For what right had she to talk so to him? What business was it of his, whether Waters was hanged or not? What business was it of any of us?

He recovered, after a time, and all through the rest of that afternoon he worked silently at his job—the hardest job of all—rolling bales. He said not a word. He was strong as two lions. And we knew it was the fire and the anger inside him that gave him the power.

But it was a miserable business. About four o'clock something happened to the beater. It stuck halfway down the box, and the power driver, after he had tried to lift it up or beat it down, gave up and yelled out:

"Chip! Hey, Chip!"

The feeder stuck his head around and says with a sort of scared, glad look:

"Is Chip coming? Where's Chip?"

The boss stepped out from the dog-house and gave the two of them a black look. Then he climbed up there and took a look at the jam.

He fumbled here, and he fumbled there, while the rest of us just sat around in what shade we could find, and the drops oozed slowly down our faces and the backs of our necks.

We sort of knew that the boss could do nothing with the

71

mess. And we knew just as well that Chip, if he had been there, could have fixed the thing in a jiffy.

He would have been down there in the box, swearing a good deal, and then singing out for tools of one kind or another, and pretty soon the business would have been done. Ten minutes, and the press would have been going again.

But Chip was not there! What a hole that left in our organization, and right between wind and water!

The chief did not talk. He just got big monkey wrenches and began to unscrew the nuts in order to take out the side of the machine.

We all helped him. We worked until dark, hardly making headway, though it was a job that we used to get through fast enough, when Chip was there to sting us with a wasp word now and again, and call us empty heads, and duffers, and what-not. Finally we got enough of the thing dismantled to see that we were all wrong.

The beater was stuck on the other side!

When we discovered this, we gave up with a groan. We turned around and went off for the cook house, though there was still a working hour left to the day. But, somehow, a general and a sudden disgust struck all of us, and we just walked off.

I looked over my shoulder and saw Newbold staring after us, with an eight-pound wrench in his big grip.

Ordinarily, he would have come after us like a tiger, but the tiger was gone out of Newbold. Something had happened to him—and I knew what it was! His heart was aching, and so was his soul, and his pride was burning him to a smoke, a red smoke.

I made note, then, not to cross that fellow in word or deed for a month, at least! He was poison now.

Even with the rest of us gone, there was no giving up for Newbold. No, sir. He stuck to his guns, and presently we could hear how he was working away at the farther side of the machine.

There he worked on and on, the two big bolts groaning and yelling out as he struggled with them. And then there were creaking, and jarring, and crashing sounds, as he struggled.

We went in for supper. The cook banged the pan three

72

times, but Newbold, working out there by lantern light, did not seem to hear.

I felt a pang of pity, but I said nothing. Nobody else spoke, either, except Bramble, who started to tell one of his best stories, about a wrangle he got into down in Veracruz, in the middle of a revolution. But nobody even pretended to listen to Bramble. He was a good fellow, was Pete, and he talked mighty well; but the point was that we all felt something extraordinarily important was happening right at our elbows, and we wanted to pay attention to that thing!

Poor old Newbold!

The memories of his hard-headedness, and harder hands, his stingy portions, his slave-driving, all began to disappear from my mind. All I could remember was that he never deserted us in a pinch, that he was a roof over us and a shield before us, in a time of danger, and that he never asked from another man one half of what he demanded from himself. Well, I had all these things in mind, and I was amazed to feel the way that my heart was softening toward him.

After supper, the racket out at the hay press stopped. The boys were lying around and smoking, and taking things easy, when one of them sang out that the hay was on fire near the press.

He'd no sooner said that, than flames ran up that press from the bottom to the top, and wagged their heads far in the sky above it. And not a man ran out to stop the conflagration, because we understood in one flash.

Newbold had tried to make the repairs, and he had failed.

And, having failed, he finally was taken by a great disgust, and he had simply doused the whole machine with oil and laid a match to it.

I ran out, with the others. They looked for the fire, but I looked for a hotter thing than that. Newbold, I mean. I couldn't see him. He was out of the way.

Then, far off on the rounding cheek of the world, I saw a glint of the dancing firelight that fell on the shadow of a rider heading off away from us.

"Newbold" said I to my heart. And my heart gave a jump and a boom that I could hear as plain as a drumbeat. "Newbold!"

I snaked out the best horse I could lay my hands on, and I sloped across that country as fast as I could go. I didn't try to follow the trail of Newbold. I knew where he was heading, and I streaked for that.

He was going to Manorville, because that was where the jail stood; and in that jail would be Waters; and near that jail would be Chip; and toward the same spot the thoughts of Marian Wray would be turning.

I had cotton in my throat, I tell you, and couldn't swallow. I was dizzy. There was something biblical about the whole affair. Like the ruin of Lot. I mean to say—an accumulation of thunderstrokes.

Why, Newbold had been the pillar of the law. Newbold had fought with that hay press as if with a sword. Newbold had hated women—or not even thought of them. Newbold never had gone from his way an inch except when one of his own men was in trouble. But now for a girl's sake he junked the press and was riding to break jail for an outlaw he despised!

I knew it, from a distance. I did not have to have his voice to tell me so. So I took a short cut, and I burned up that mustang humping across the flat, and soaring over the hills, till at last I got to a small hummock and could look down onto the widening main road to Manorville; and there below me, coming along at a singing gallop, was a horseman so tall that he made his horse look small.

Newbold, I knew!

I jabbed the spurs into the tired sides of that horse of mine and gave it pain or courage to take the slide. Down it went, and we slid out onto the road in a shower of gravel, and small stones, and sand, and I ranged alongside of Newbold.

He didn't even glance at me. No, you might have thought that he was alone, and that nothing had happened worth seeing or hearing, until we came to an up-pitch in the grade, and he said to me, as the horses fell to a walk:

"Joe!"

"Ay?" said I.

"What do you gain out of this?" he asked me. "What do you buy?"

"Me? Nothing," I said.

He nodded. I could see him nodding in the dark.

74

"You go home," said he.

"That's all right," said I. "I'll stay along, I guess!"

He didn't argue. He wasn't a fellow to argue, except with his fists.

But, after a while, we topped that rise, and we saw the scattering lights of Manorville with blank darkness between them, here and there, like bald spots on the head of a bleak old man.

There he reined his horse to a stop, and I thought he was changing his mind. At last he said:

"Look how many years I've been!"

"Been what?" said I.

"A hound!" said he.

Chapter Fifteen

One cannot make an answer to a remark like that. So I didn't try, and we rode on into Manorville. It was a strange feeling that I had. A feeling, you see, of guilt; but of a prospective rather than present guilt. For the moment, no one could say to me that I had violated the law. Never in my life! It was a sweet feeling, too, to be able to walk along the streets and know that I was the honest peer of every man I faced. And yet, was I the honest peer, after all? No, because the guilt was already in my heart!

Well, we decided that the first thing to do was to look things over. In case there was any action, it would be better to have our horses out of sight. So we put up our mustangs on the edge of the town that was nearest to the jail. Then we walked in. We'd left the horses in a scrub of small trees, where they could smell out the grass that grew in between, and that grass grew thick enough to content them, of course. It doesn't take much to content a range-bred mustang.

We went in past the jail itself. There was only one window that showed light on our side, and it was a gloomy flickering light.

75

Said the boss:

"That's a lantern, and a smoking lantern, that's inside. And it's fouling the air a good deal with its smoking old wick."

I knew he didn't care a rap what sort of a lantern was burning in yonder. He was only interested in the job that he had before him, but he took it out on small things. His heart was aching a good deal, I suppose. At last I couldn't hold in, and I said:

"Newbold, you're making this play for the girl. What's your surety that she'll do anything for you if you win?"

I expected him to grow angry at this remark, but he merely said:

"Shut up, and keep out of my business. I'm not sure about anything. And I'm doing it for Chip, more'n the girl. Chip—he's worth more than any ten men I ever saw!"

I was half inclined to agree with this remark, but still I knew, of course, that he was lying. Poor Newbold!

We wanted to pick up what information we could, and so we sauntered on together into the lighted part of town —there was only two blocks of it. I saw "Pie" Lafferty of the Crippled Star outfit. I never knew where they got that name for their brand. Any name would have done for the wicked scroll they used. Pie was half tight and shining like a full moon. He insisted on coming along with us, until he luckily met another friend in the next half block and switched to him.

So I went on with the boss. We passed the hotel, and just as we passed it, down the steps came— Who do you think? Why, down those steps came Marian Wray and Chip!

When Chip saw us, he grabbed the arms of the girl and she turned, too, and the pair of them gave us a stare. I would have stopped, but Newbold walked straight on, as though he had not seen a thing. His jaw was locked hard. He was looking before him, and seeing nothing—as I knew by the way he stumbled.

Then a hand touched my arm, and it was Chip, saying:

"Good old Joe! I knew that you would figger into this, somehow. You wouldn't go and leave him lay!"

"Chip," said I, "what's the deal, so far?"

"Here comes Marian," said Chip. "Whatcha think?

76

She ain't just a fool girl. She's all right! She's about a hundred per cent. Here she comes!"

She came up. And she was shining brighter than Pie Lafferty, and almost the same red. She didn't say a word, that girl. She just looked!

No, sir, there was the most chipper and cock-sure girl I ever saw in my life, and the wordiest, and the most free and easy, and the most on top of the world, but all that she did was to stand there like a fifteen-year-old sweetheart and blush, by thunder, and widen her eyes, and look up, and smile at Newbold!

Yes, and that leather-necked, hard-headed, iron-hearted Newbold—why, he fairly shook in his boots! He weakened right then and there so far that I knew he never would recover. He would go ahead and be a hero and get himself busted in the face with a load of buckshot, or some such thing. But a hero he would certainly be.

Chip grabbed my arm again.

"Newbold's gone nutty," said he, "and so's the girl. Look at her, now. That's the effect that a woman has even on a man like him. Kind of softening. It's a sad thing, Joe, the way that a girl with her fool smiling soaks right through the outside lining of a man and gets at the inners of him. Now, you and me have gotta plan something and put our heads together. Newbold, he'll just be a pair of hands, and no more."

I nodded. The blank look on Newbold's face promised nothing at all. I would as soon have asked advice from a flounder as a word from him. He was just looking at that girl and seeing heaven in Manorville.

Chip and I went back up the street.

"If he comes far enough to find us," said Chip, "all right. But if he don't, he'd only be a burden on us."

"Look here, Chip," said I. "You don't think that I'm going to take a main hand in this without the boss, do you? I'm only the second assistant. I'm not the straw boss, here."

"Oh, I know you, old Joe," said Chip. "You're a lot bigger hoss than you give yourself the credit of being. I know you pretty well, old son. You'd win a mighty lot of races, if only you'd enter yourself in 'em!"

He had a cheerful way about him, that brat. It started

a man's circulation along to hear him talk. Then he started planning what we ought to do.

He had looked over the place pretty thoroughly, he said. And the best way that he could figure out was to try through the roof. For there was a tree to the rear of the jail that extended a branch over the top of the jail, and by climbing out upon the branch, he could easily drop or slip down onto the roof, probably without making a sound.

Then he could work on the skylight, and with any sort of a small jimmy he could pry the skylight loose; and, after that, it ought to be easy to get down to the block of the cells.

"But what'll be done when you get there?" asked I. "There still would be cell doors to open, wouldn't there?"

"Sure there would," said he.

"And guards with guns, and everything?" I suggested, more blankly than ever.

"There's one guard," said the boy confidently, "and that's what I'm counting on. He'll have the keys to the cells. You and me, we sneak down in there, and I make a noise and get the guard's eye on me. He asks me what the deuce I'm doing there; and while he's asking, you slip up behind and get him with a strangle hold, and I ram a gun into his stomach and ask him to come to time. He'll come to time, all right. I've seen him, and he's one of those fellows that's got himself a big, rough reputation by shooting some poor stiff that was already blind in both eyes with whisky. Now he lives on what he's done, and looks black, and gives three chaws to his quid before he answers a word from anybody except the sheriff. But he's yaller, or I never seen yaller."

I nodded. But I wasn't convinced.

Chip kept insisting:

"What you think, Joe? If that ain't a good plan, what plan is good? You name one, and it'll do for me! But we gotta do something quick. There's a lot of interest taken in this town about the poor Chief. And there's a lot of things that's been blamed on him, from burglary to dog stealin', that he never done in his lifetime. They're standin' together, the boys down there in the street, like a lot of chickens on a cold day, and they're workin' up a lot of heat about Waters. It's a handy thing to have a man ready

78

for lynchin', in a cheap town like this. And pretty soon they're gunna come and stretch Waters's neck for him, unless we look sharp."

"We'd better wait for Newbold," said I.

"There's no use waiting," sighed the boy. "He's gone and paralyzed himself looking at the girl. And she's gone and paralyzed herself admirin' of how Newbold has come into town. How come he to bust away from the hay press as long as this, tell me?"

"There's no hay press any more," said I. "The boss burned it before we started for town."

"Burned it?" exclaimed Chip. "He burned that press? Why, it was a mighty good little old press, only it needed some understanding. That was all it needed. You gotta favor a Little Giant press, sometimes, but they turn out the boss bales and the handiest in the world. You can break 'em over the knees, because they stand the highest."

He was very indignant.

He was still pressing me to suggest a new plan or else to offer one of my own, when a man walked down the street with a long, stalking stride and headed straight for the jail.

At the same time, there was a sudden yipping from the direction of the hotel, and looking down that way, we could see a couple of dozen men spill out into the lighted part of the street; and every one of those men was carrying a gun!

Then I could see that the boy was right. Lynching was what the rascals intended. And the thought took my breath like a jump into ice-cold water.

"Now—quick!" said Chip, and tugged at my arms.

I hardly knew what to do, but I started vaguely along with him. At the same time, the silhouette of the tall man with the long step went up to the front door of the jail and banged on it.

"By Jiminy," said Chip, "ain't that Newbold?"

I stopped and stared.

"It can't be," said I. "There's not even a mask on his face. He wouldn't go and tap on the door of the jail, like that, without a mask on his face!"

"Wouldn't he?" snarled Chip, with a whine of joy in his voice. "I've seen whisky drunks do worse than that, and a girl drunk is worse than a whisky one! It's New-bold!"

It was Newbold. I could see the labor-stoop of his shoulders, and the long swing of his arms at his sides.

The door of the jail opened a crack; then Newbold jerked it wide with a single thrust and dived into the inside darkness. We heard some one yell.

And in the meantime, Chip was streaking it for the danger point, and I had to lumber along behind, trying to swallow down my heart and not managing to do it.

Well, we got to that jail door just as the crowd down the street near the hotel marshaled itself and let out a few whoops, and then started marching to make trouble; every minute it was getting bigger, as men, and boys, and even women, ran out from their houses to join in the main body or the flanks. Nobody in Manorville wanted to miss fun as good as this.

But Chip and I, as we entered the jail, heard scuffling and cursing on the pitch-dark floor of the jail, and not a thing except a sense of touch to show us what was happening.

Chapter Sixteen

I would not have known what to do, but Chip did not hesitate. He simply dived into the darkness of the floor as though it were water, and I heard the voice of big Newbold greeting him with a growl of satisfaction.

Evidently, Chip was already helping.

I got a match lighted, and the glimpse which it gave me showed that same jailer, the one whom Chip disapproved of as a brute and a bully, with red running from several cuts on his bulldog face, trying, like a bulldog, to snap at his annoyers with his teeth, since his arms were imprisoned and anchored.

Newbold held him. Chip vainly threatened him with a gun, but the fellow was regardless, fearless, heroic. I suppose Chip had known very well beforehand just what he would be, but had wanted to encourage me as much as he could.

A lantern was rolling with a jangle on the floor, and I picked it up and lighted it. At the same time, there was a wail and a yell of joy from half a dozen voices inside that jail.

Waters was not the only prisoner, d'you see, and the others were tuning up like roosters that think the day has come.

Newbold was free, now, for he had twisted a length of cord around the wrists of the jail guard and turned him face down on the floor.

"Keep your eyes shut. Don't turn your head," said Newbold, "or you'll be slammed!" He beckoned to me.

So I took my place there and just tapped the muzzle of my revolver against the base of the guard's skull.

"Look here, brother," I told him truthfully. "I'm not one of those heroes that won't take an advantage. You try to turn your head and get a look at me or the others, and I'll just slam a bullet right through your brain."

It was a wonderful thing to watch that fellow. I never saw more natural fighting instinct, for as he lay there, he whined and whimpered, on my word of honor, exactly like a dog that wants to fight and is held on a leash. So I kept talking to him, gently, and tapping him with that gun to keep him quiet.

All the while he gritted his teeth, and his big shoulder muscles worked. He cursed and whined and cursed again. He was fairly trembling with a desire to get up and resume the fight. It was no wonder that this fellow had opened the door of the jail at the first summons. For he didn't care a rap if there were trouble waiting outside the door. Why should he? He would welcome it; and the more trouble, the more welcome!

I never saw such a man. He gave my flesh the creeps!

In the meantime, Chip had got hold of the keys from the guard; and he was flinging down the corridor of the little cells until he came to the farthest one in the corner, and he started to try them in the lock, one after the other.

I thought he was taking until the end of the world to do this, because all the time I could hear the moan and the roar of the crowd which was coming up the street.

Have you ever heard that murmur of rising human tides? It's not so easy to listen to. It keeps creeping higher and higher in the throat, until the back of your tongue is glued against the roof of your mouth.

But finally the right key was found, and the iron hinges of the cell door groaned as it swung open.

Through it came Waters. The lantern light gleamed on his face. One high light lay like a ghostly finger on his temple, and his sunken cheek was marked by shadow as by soot.

Big Newbold took him under the armpits and fairly swept him through the doorway. Chip was dancing before them. And the rest of the thugs in the jail, seeing that they were not going to be turned free in the jail break, howled like rabid wolves. Hai! How their voices went through me!

I was the last to go through the door of the jail, pulling it shut with a slam behind me, and with the others before me, and the crowd breaking into a run straight at us, from down the street, I circled around toward the corner of the jail.

I knew that we were goners. Or at least, I thought that we were goners, because certainly we could not run fast enough, with Waters for a hand-burden, to keep away from the stretching hands of that rabble of man hunters.

But then little Chip, at the corner of the building, whirled around, and he let out a screech like a wild cat that's had its tail stepped on, and at the same time he snatches out a mansized Colt and lets fly at that crowd!

Right at them, I thought at the moment, though I was wrong. He was only shooting for the ground at their feet. However, the crowd was even more convinced than I, by that maniacal screech from the boy, and I suppose that when the bullets kicked the dust up into the faces of the leaders, they had enough on the spot.

For they stopped. Mind you, that young split of Satan stopped the whole crowd with three bullets; and with three more he scattered them yelling to either side, hunting for safety, convinced that the desperadoes meant murder!

That was how we got to the horses, and with the horses we went out of Manorville in one direction; and the man hunt went roaring, and shouting, and gloriously whooping in another direction.

So everybody was happy!

I was about the least happy of the lot. There was one thing that I specially hated, and that thing was the shadow of the law. I didn't want any part or parcel of it. I wanted to be clean free from it. And here I was with tar on the tips of my fingers!

By the next day, however, we knew that the lay of the land was unbelievably good.

Waters and Chip faded off through the hills in one direction, and the boss and I went home in another; and by noon of the next day came the story about the jail break—but no warrant for our arrest along with it!

And then over to the camp comes the girl with the final word. Yes, I've got to say that Marian Wray lived up to any unspoken promise that she had given to the boss. She came right over, where we were cleaning up happily the wreck of that danged hay press, and she went up to Newbold and kissed him—*bang!*—right in front of everybody. And she came over and kissed me, too, though any one could see the difference.

She took us each under her arm, so to speak, and while the rest of the boys gaped after us, pretty enviously, she walked off with us and told us what had happened. And that was this: That everybody in Manorville knew Newbold, and, therefore, everybody in the town knew that he could not have been the wild man of the jail break! Nobody dreamed of recognizing him as the great desperado.

Nobody noticed me, either, I suppose, because my part was so small. Only it was known that two tall men, and one short one—they called Chip a man!—had turned the trick. And there you are! And the shadow of the law slipped right off my shoulders!

And I saw before me a good break, and a chance at a happy life once more, and that sun-flaming, sun-wrecked cow range, it looked to me like cool blue heaven, you can bet.

I stepped aside and let the boss go on, slowly, with Marian Wray at his side, half turning, looking up to him, laughing.

Only Chip—what would become of him and his outlaw?

Well, nothing bad, at least. Because only good can come out of good in the end.

PART TWO

Chapter One

Every man has a special country that is fitted into his heart so snugly that it fills every corner. I know fellows who talk pretty nearly with tears in their eyes of the seashore, and the white curving of the surf, and the boom and the step of it; but they never can outtalk the lads from the high mountains, where the head and shoulders of things is lifted up so high that it almost breaks loose.

Then I've heard the real Kentuckian mention blue grass and big hills that never stop rolling from one edge of the sky to the other; yes, I've heard 'em mention blue grass, and horses, too.

Up there in New England things are smaller and put together more closely, but summer mugginess and flies and winter chilblains and wind can't stop the New Englander from talking. He'll tell you about a second growth forest, and the smell of the moldering stumps in it, and the autumn colors slashed through it like paint flung off a brush; and he'll talk of the brook where it runs, and the brook where it stands still and lets a couple of silver birches look down into it to see how much sky is there.

Then you'll hear people even rave a lot about sagebrush, and the smell of the wind that comes off from it when it's wet, but for me there's only one land that I feel God made when He was working in real earnest. The other parts of the world—well, He just made 'em for practice, but finally He got really interested, and then He made Nevada.

Yes, I mean that. Maybe I'm not talking about the part you know, because a lot of people are loaded right down to the water line with wrong information about that State. There's a sort of a general impression that there's some silver mining and sage hens in it, but they've got to scratch their heads to remember anything else.

Well, there's too much Nevada for the people who live there to talk about. There's about a couple of square miles of space for every hombre in that country—yes, man, woman, and child. And when you realize that mostly everybody is raked together in a few towns and mining camps, you'll see that it's possible to bump right into a lot of open space out in that direction.

I've bumped into it, boys. I've ridden it from the Opal Mountains to Massacre Lakes, and from Goose Greek Range to Lake Tahoe, and wondered how there could be that much real, fresh, sweet cold water in the world. And I know the ranges that sink their claws into the hide of Nevada, like the Monitor and Pancake and Hot Creek and Toiyabe and Shoshone and Augusta. I know that whole State. I know the dry feel of it on the skin, and the red hurt of it in the eyes. And I love it. There's salt in my throat when I think of Nevada, but I love it, and I hope that I'll live there and die there, God bless it!

But now I've got to particularize a little. You may have sage flats in your mind, but that's not the part of Nevada that I mean. No, sir; I mean the place where God really turned Himself loose and did His best. He didn't waste any time picking and choosing. He just reached out with both hands, and He piled up all kinds of slates and limestones and quartzites and granites, and for color He piled in some volcanic rocks that are some of them as blue as the sky, and some of them as red as fire.

He worked with this stuff and threw it up into great ridges and He chopped out the valley with the edge of His palm. He made things ragged, and He made things grand. He didn't want to dull the outlines He had drawn with forests and such things. He wanted no beard on the face that He'd made; He preferred it clean-shaven, so He reached over to the westward, and He ridged up the Sierra Nevadas. There's quite a lot of people in the State of Oranges and Hot Air—California, I mean—that think that the Sierra Nevadas were built up for their own special satisfaction, a kind of a wall and a turning of the back on the rest of the world; but really the only reason that the Sierras are up so high is to catch all the rain winds out of the westerly and pick out the mists and the clouds so that only a pure, dry air can blow over Nevada. God didn't want those Nevada mountains and valleys to rust in the rain.

Well, when He'd finished off the main outlines, He says to Himself that He might give a few finishing touches, so He paved the valleys with fine white sand, and He polished up the mountains so that they'd shine, night and day. And then He says to Himself that this is the finest spot on earth, and what will He put into it?

Well, He finally picked out the jack rabbit that was biggest and fastest, and it could clear a mountain in its stride; and then He hunted up some coyotes that could run the rabbits down; and after that He got the wisest beast in the world, a big frame and a loose hide, and an eye like a man's eye, and He put the gray wolf into the picture and yellowed and grayed it a good deal to make it fit in with the landscape better. Here and there He let a four-footed streak of greased lightning step through those valleys on tiptoe, and those antelope are the fastest and the wisest of their silly, beautiful kind. On the ground He laid rattlesnakes to catch fools, such as you and I, and in the air He put the sage thrasher and the Texas nighthawk, and the mourning dove, and in every sky He hung one buzzard.

Now He wanted to get some people in there to see all this picture, but He didn't want many. So He just sifted into the rocks of His mountains some gold and silver, here and there. It wasn't much. It was a trace. Just enough to make your mouth water, and not hardly enough to swallow. But the prospectors got the wind of it, and they came ten thousand miles across the world to have a look. Mostly they turned back on the rim of the picture—it was too black and white for them, and all the white was fire. The thermometer was ranging a hundred and fifty degrees in the year, and some had their hearts burned out, and some had their feet frozen. But a few went on in.

They climbed up onto the shoulders of those mountains and thanked God for a piñon, now and then; even the

87

greasewood, and the creosote bushes and the sage seemed like company out there. They found their leads, and they sank their shafts into hard ground and banged and hammered all day long. They got mighty little, and they knew, mostly, that there wasn't much hope. But still they felt mighty contented.

Why?

Well, it might have been because of the mornings, before they started to work and let their eyes go sinking over the white valleys, or the mountains beginning to tremble and blush in the early light. Or it might have been because of the evenings, when they sat dead tired and smoked their pipes, and looked at the evening rising just like a blue smoke out of the bottom of the rifts.

That was what I was doing.

I was just sitting there in front of my claim and figuring out that I had used up my last can of tomatoes, and sort of cussing a little, quietly and comfortably, all to myself; but my brain didn't hear what my lips were muttering, do you see, because I was too really busy taking gun shots down one ravine filled with that blue smoke, and then down another choked with fire. And the white of the valley floor was still pure and very little clouded, and away off on the vanishing edge of things I could see a slowly moving cloud.

It was a dust cloud. It was raised by wild horses. I had seen them that morning, looking through that glass-clear air. During the night they would pass me, but on the following morning I would be able to see them again, traveling on at their unfailing lope in a two-day run to the water holes of the Shoe Horn Valley, away beyond.

I remember thinking of the wild horses, that I'd like to be out on the back of one of them, the wildest stallion of the lot, and go flowing on with the dusty stream of their march, and stay with them forever, contented. I mean to say, I felt that I was only sitting still on the bank of the river, looking; but those horses were in the river, they were in the picture, they were a part of it.

While I was thinking these things over, a voice says behind me:

"Why, hello, old Joe!"

I just pulled myself a little closer together. I looked up, but I was afraid to look behind.

"I've got them!" I said to myself.

I mean, when you're out all alone for too long a stretch, sometimes the brain wabbles a little, and you'll find a prospector turn as batty as a sheep-herder. For surely that voice I heard could not have come from any human lips. That boy Chip was likely to be anywhere, but he simply couldn't have materialized there at my back.

I laughed a little, with a quiver in my voice. "I've certainly got 'em!" said I aloud.

"Look around, Joe," said the voice again.

So I turned around and looked, and by thunder, there was the freckled face and the fire-red hair of Chip, sure enough! My heart jumped at the sight of him.

Also, my heart fell!

Chapter Two

"You little sawed-off son of salt," I said to him. "Where did you drop from?"

He hooked his thumb over his shoulder to indicate the mountainside that leaned back into the sky.

"Aw, over that way," said he.

We shook hands. He had the same hands that I remembered so well. They hadn't changed a bit; there seemed to be the same dirt darkening them around the first joints, if you know what I mean. No, all of him was just the same. He had sixteen years of growth on him, and a hundred years of sense, and a thousand years of meanness. All mixed and rolled and stewed together. Nobody ever talked down to Chip. Not more than once, I mean. One try was usually enough.

"Sit down," said I. "You just walked out here a few hunderd miles and found me, eh? No trouble to you. What did you do? Learn the buzzard language and ask the birds which way to go?"

He sat down on the ground, laid his back against a rock, and folded his arms under his head. He was facing partly away from me, so that he could look at the same picture which I was seeing.

"Make me a smoke, Joe, will you?" says he.

I was about to throw him the makings and tell him to roll his own, when I saw that he was dead tired. There were violet shadows thumbed out under his eyes. Besides, just the asking for a cigarette was enough to show that he was beat. He didn't smoke them often.

So I rolled him tobacco and wheat straw, and stuck it in his mouth and lighted it for him; and he didn't budge a hand, but just lay there with his eyes half closed and looked at the picture in front of us.

The poor kid was almost all in. I said nothing for a time. I simply watched him, do you see? He smoked that cigarette to a butt and jerked it out, and he breathed deep three times before the smoke was entirely out of his lungs.

Then I said: "You've gone and got yourself a whole flock of new clothes since I saw you last."

"Yeah," said he, "you know the way Dug is. He's always trying to dress me up."

"Yeah. I know," said I.

"That's the trouble with Dug," said the kid. "He's kind of a dude."

"Yeah. He's kind of a dude," said I, "but he's all right."

"Yeah, sure, he's all right," said the kid. "But he's a dude. He's always fixing himself up and dressing up. You know what he did down in Tahuila?"

"What did he go and do there?" I asked.

"He done himself up in Mexican clothes. All velvet and such stuff. And he went and got a big plume to curl around his head. He thought he looked fine. He was always standing around and spreading his legs and looking at himself in the mirror and curling his whiskers with one hand."

"I bet you handed him something," said I.

"Yeah. I handed him something," said Chip. "But he didn't care. He's getting so he don't care what I say to him."

"He knows you kind of like him," said I.

"Think that's it?" said he.

"Yeah. That's it," said I.

"Well, maybe," said Chip.

I swallowed a smile. He and Dug Waters were closer than brothers. I was pretty thick with them, too. But what they meant to one another was real blood. They'd owed their lives, each to each, I don't know how many times.

"What did he do when he got all dressed up?" said I.

"Aw, he goes and crashes into a dance," said Chip.

"Did they try to throw him out?" said I.

"Yeah, they tried," said Chip, and yawned heartily. He went on: "He stayed quite a while, though. The furniture got sort of busted up, and his fine clothes were spoiled, but he kept the music playing, and he kept on dancing. I gave him the sign when the cops were coming, and then he left. But that's the trouble with him. He's always dressing up. You know how it is. You always get into trouble when you're dressed up."

"How'd you lose half of those suspenders?" I asked him.

"That was a shack," said Chip. "He reached for me as I was getting off the back end of the caboose on a grade. He got half the suspenders, but he didn't get me."

"That's good," said I. "How about the sleeve of the shirt? What happened to that?"

"A funny thing about that," said Chip. "The railroad cop, when he grabbed me, he grabbed so hard that when I popped out of my coat I had to tear that sleeve right out of the shirt, too, before I could shake him. You never seen a guy with a grip like that cop had."

"Where was this?" I asked.

"Aw, in a railroad yard," said Chip. "This was one of them mean cops. You know the real mean ones?"

"Yeah. I know."

"He comes cruising up to me in the dark," said Chip. "He makes a pass at me, and all his fingers are fishhooks, what I mean to say. He grabs me and he holds me. I have to peel out of the coat and the shirt sleeve. The talking that cop done as he heeled after me, you'd've laughed to've heard it, Joe."

He himself smiled faintly, a little wearily, at the memory.

"That was hard on the shirt, all right," said I. "You got a pretty bad rip in those trousers too."

One side of them was almost torn away, and had been loosely patched together with sack twine.

"You know how it is about a window?" said Chip. "I mean, the nails that are always sticking out around a window? That was what happened. I was clean through and ready to drop for the ground, and nobody had heard a thing, and then I got hung up on a nail. It makes me pretty dog-gone sore, Joe, the way carpenters make a window. Dog-gone me, if I was a carpenter and called myself a carpenter, and set up for being a carpenter, I'd be one, and I'd hammer in my nails, and I'd countersink 'em—around a window, anyways."

He was very indignant. His anger helped to take his weariness away.

"Yeah," I said. "Carpenters are no good. Who'd want to be a carpenter, anyway? But what window were you climbing out of?"

"Aw, it was nothing," said he carelessly. "It was just a bet I had on with Dug Waters. He said I couldn't break into a house. I said I could."

I began to perspire a little.

"What did you get, Chip?" said I.

He turned his head quickly and glanced at me.

"Whatcha think?" said he. "I ain't in that line. I never ain't going to be in it, either, what's more."

"That's right," said I. "You're a good kid, Chip."

"Aw, go on. I ain't a good kid, either," said he. "But I ain't a thief. I don't go around stealing. That's all I don't do."

"Just a chicken now and then?" said I.

"That's lifting. That ain't stealing," said Chip calmly. "You oughta know the difference between lifting and stealing, oughtn't you?"

"Sure," said I. "There's a lot of difference. How do you feel, now?"

"Me? I always feel good," said he. "How about you?"

"I'm all right. I'm just kind of down now, because I've used up my tomatoes."

"Have you?" said Chip. "Well, you're gonna get some more."

"When?" I asked him.

"Pronto," said he.

And he held up one finger to make me listen. I heard

it, then. It was the thin, silver music of a bell, beyond the shoulder of the hill.

"What's that?" I asked him.

"That's my hoss and mule," said Chip.

"Oh," said I. "Then Dug Waters is coming after you, is he?"

"No," said Chip.

"Who's with 'em, then?" I asked.

"Nobody's with 'em," said he. "There're by themselves."

I looked at him pretty hard, but he paid no attention, as though there were nothing really worthy of attention in what he had said. He merely looked off across the blue and red of the evening, toward one great polished face of granite which took the light and gave it back as a mirror would.

"Maybe you've worked a charm on 'em?" said I. "And they can't help following you?"

"I got a charm, all right," said he. "I got the meanest mustang in the world, all right. He's a charm! But he'll follow me. He'll follow me around like a dog, because he gets pretty lonely without me. He don't feel nacheral at all without somebody in the saddle that he can annoy a little. If it ain't bucking, it's reaching around and taking a bite at my foot; and if there's a cliff handy, he likes to walk right out onto the edge of nothing and bite a couple of chunks out of it, and he don't turn back until the cliff is crumblin' under his feet, and even then, he don't hurry. Then he likes to give me a rub against a handy boulder along the way, that cayuse does. And if he ain't bucking, he's always humping his back like he was about to begin, so's your nerves never get good and settled down.

"He's so fond of makin' me miserable that he can't do without me. I'm his kicking post, and he certainly likes to kick. He's lammed me three times on this trip, and he's gonna lam me three times more; and I've seen the air around my head all full of his heels. That's the kind of a mustang that he is! He can't do without me. So I know that he'll follow me, because he's got a gift of scenting like a wolf, and so I hang a bell around his neck; and the mule is an old train mule, and follows that bell like it was a bag of oats. And when I get tired of fighting the cayuse, I hop off and take a walk ahead, like now, and he's sure to come after me. First he balks, and pretends that he ain't coming, but when he remembers what a lot of fun he's had pounding me, he always gives in and comes along after."

When Chip got through with this explanation, over the shoulder of the mountain, between two runty piñons, I saw the procession coming, the little mustang first, and a longlegged, knock-kneed, pot-bellied mule behind him.

That cayuse came up, and my burro began to bray, it was so glad of having company. Right up to Chip that mustang came, and reaches down and takes off the battered old felt hat that Chip is wearing.

"Aw, quit it," says Chip, without turning his head, and sort of tired. "Quit it, and go off and lay down, or I'll get up and slam you one."

Well, it amused me a good deal to see the mustang drop the hat and go off to the side to pick at some bunch grass. It amused me, because it seemed as though he had understood.

He was the meanest-looking horse that I ever saw, with a Roman nose, and a red look about the eye; and there was that hump in the back that always means a hard gait and a mighty good bucker.

"How'd you come to pick out that horse, Chip?" said I.

"Out of a hundred," said Chip. "I could have had my pick of the whole bunch; but while I was looking, there was a fight started in the corral between a great big sixteen-hand bay, with quarters like a dray horse, and this little runt. And they just backed up against one another and let drive. Every time the bay kicked I looked to see the runt exploded right off the face of the earth, like gunpowder. But every time it kicked, its fool heels flew over the back of the cayuse, and every time the cayuse kicked, its feet went into the big fat quarters of that bay like a clapping of hands. After a while the bay had enough, begun to squeal and run away, and this little wild cat run after him, and took out a chunk with his teeth while the bay was running. 'Shoot that blankety-blank hoss-eating mustang!' yells the boss. 'No,' I says, 'sell it to me!' So that's how I got him."

I got through laughing, and I said: "Where are you bound, and what for, Chip?"

"I'm bound to you from Waters," said he. "Take off that saddlebag and you'll see why."

I went over and navigated around the bronco until I got the saddlebag off. I brought it back and opened it, and dumped out the contents on the ground; and what I saw was a whole stack of packs of cards, except that they were bigger than packs of cards, and at the ends of them I could see the figures.

And all at once I threw up my hands and let out a howl, because I knew that all that stuff was United States green-backs, lying there on the rocks before me!

Chapter Three

Sometimes I had daydreamed about how good it would be if I could run into a flock of money like that—sort of have it poured down before me by the dropping of the tailpiece of a government truck, or something like that. I had always felt that the joy would run up through my veins as bright as silver.

But I was wrong.

At least, out there in the center of the Nevada desert, the first thing that I did was to throw a look around over both shoulders, and the second thing was to go and grab my rifle and shove some cartridges into it.

Even then I didn't feel very easy, because my hands were shaking, and I was as cold as ice all around my mouth. My voice quaked when I came back to Chip and stood over him.

"You little son of torment!" said I to him.

He only grinned at me.

"Gimme the makings, Joe," says he.

"You don't smoke till you've done some talking," says I.

He grinned again. He settled himself back against the rock as though it were a pillow and folded his arms under his head, with his skinny elbows sticking out on either side.

"Go on," said he. "What d'you wanta know?"

"Everything," said I.

"That's easy," says the kid. "Once upon a time there was a bank, and inside of the bank there was a president that knew how to suck the gold out of people like a spider does blood out of flies, and inside of the president's office there was a safe all bright and shining and new and guaranteed, where the president laid up the gold. And now there's the same bank, and the same president, and the same safe. But there ain't any door onto the safe. Leastwise, there wasn't the last time I saw it. And a couple hundred thousand dollars' worth of lining is gone, too, right out of the president's safekeeping."

All the rocks and the mountains shifted and wavered a little as I heard this. I looked down at the little pile I had turned out of the saddlebag.

"Two—hundred—thousand!" said I.

"Yeah. Or nigher onto a quarter of a million," says the kid.

I looked at the loot again.

It didn't seem to me like stolen money. It seemed different; I can't say why. Because there was so much of it, that it seemed almost right and good to have taken it. I thought of a lump of gold weighing eight hundred pounds. It would load down two mules solid. And that was what that little stack of paper meant. It was a treasure. That's what I thought of it.

Murder came hot up in me. I want to be honest and tell the horrible truth about it. I had half of a mind to tap the boy over the head with the butt of the rifle and then all of this money would be mine. I took my knuckles a good hard swipe across my forehead, and then my brain was clear, and I was able to think and see right again.

I found that Chip was stretched out there in just the same position, looking up at me with a funny little smile.

He nodded. "Yeah, I know," said he.

"Do you?" said I, and I stared down, and saw that his bright, wise eyes were full of information and understanding.

"Yeah," went on Chip. "I had the same idea. When I started away, I was a mind to cut and run, and never see Waters again if I could help it. But then I remembered, and didn't."

"Remembered that he'd track you down?" I asked.

"No. I remembered that he wouldn't try," said Chip.

I let this idea go through me with an electric jump, and I saw that it was true. After all that Chip had done for Waters, Dug never would lay a hand on him, no matter what else he did. Not for a quarter of a million in hard cash.

"How did he do the trick?" I asked the boy.

"How did he do it? Oh, that was easy. He just chloroformed a watchman and cut his way in, and cut his way out. It was an easy job. That bank had plate-glass windows, and you could look through them into the lighted insides of the bank, day and night, and see the safe. And the light was still shining inside the bank all that night; but Dug, he just washed a couple of the panes of the window glass with soapy water, and after that, everything you could see from the street was a mist. And he worked inside as easy as you please."

I nodded. I could see Waters, cool and easy and calm, doing his work inside the bank, with no other screen to protect him than a film of mist through which the passers-by could half see. I thought of the cleverness of it. too— people who wandered down the street that night would never give the soapy windows a thought. But a curtain or a shade drawn would have been a different matter.

"Go on," said I.

"To what?" asked Chip.

"To where you start and Dug stays back."

"Well, they guessed at Dug, and he knew that they'd guess at him," said Chip, "and just then they didn't have anything on him, but they were pretty sure to lay a slick job like that to his door. So he sat still and let them grab him and third-degree him, if they wanted to. And while they were working over him, there was me, all dressed up in a new suit of clothes, and with a good saddlebag crammed with the stuff, hiking it down the railroad. I lost some of the clothes, but I come through with the loot."

"How did you find me?" I asked.

"Well, I dropped in at Newbold's place. And Marian Newbold, she went and cried all over me. And she was going to reform me and get me sure jammed into a school this time. But I managed to find out that you were off in this direction, so I slid out at night and barged along, and the next day I bought me this outfit and hit the desert up this way. I happened onto the place where you bought your own outfit, and they gave me enough of a lead to follow along for quite a ways. The rest was luck."

I considered this for a moment. I mean to say, I thought of the nerve of Waters in trusting that fortune into the hands of the boy, and the dangers that the kid had gone through, beating his way a thousand miles, I suppose, to find me. But here he was, true as a homing pigeon, arrived at me!

It was an amazing thing. It was so amazing that I went over and unsaddled his horse and mule while I thought it over still longer. He got to his feet to help me, but I saw the waver of him through the dusk, and I told him to sit still. He could be the guest, tonight, and I'd take care of things.

I did. I dragged in the packs and the saddles under the boarding about the mouth of the shaft, and under the lean-to where I lived, though there wasn't much room in that.

Chip had brought along all the supplies in the world. There was no reason why he should have bought both a horse and a mule; but he said that he really did not know how long he would have to cruise before he found me, and so he had prepared for a voyage of any length. With his pockets full of cash, he did not spare his funds, but he laid in the best of everything.

There were the cans of tomatoes that he had promised. And I don't know anything better than canned tomatoes on a trip. They put seasoning into even the toughest old sage hen, and they make you a drink that beats beer, even— there's a good, sour bite to it. He had jams, and the best kind of white flour, and the finest bacon you ever saw, and plenty of coffee, and the little runt actually put in some pickles, too. He sure was a regular food caravan, that kid!

We ate a supper that nearly burst us both, and then we laid back, and I stoked up on my pipe and pulled off my boots, and wriggled my toes in the cool of the night breeze, and saw the stars drifting and drifting up over the mountain heads, and showing through the valley rifts, until it seemed as though they were rising out of the ground and setting into it again like undying sparks from a fire.

"Now you tell me why you're here, son," said I.

"Because it's a long time since I seen you, and I had to go somewhere," said he.

I shook my head. I looked across the deadness of the firelight to the face of the kid, and the bright glint of his eyes.

"You liar, you come clean with me," said I.

"Yeah, I'm coming clean," said Chip. "The fact is that everything looked pretty good. And then I heard that Tug Murphy had hooked into the traces and was going to work on this job."

Tug Murphy!

Dug Waters!

It was not the first time that they had tried wits against one another. And it was not the first time that Chip had thrown his weight decisively into the scale.

That Irish sheriff was not the cleverest fellow in the world, but he was a bulldog on a trail, and he was likely to get by persistence what smarter men missed, in spite of their brains. It gave me a stir to hear that name. I could see the red fighting face once more. I could hear the rasp of his voice against my ear.

"What has Murphy got to do with this game?" I asked.

"He's on the trail," said the boy. "I didn't mind the others. I would have stayed put. They wouldn't suspect me of anything. But Tug Murphy is different. He's got brains, and he knows where to look for the most trouble. So, sometimes, he might give me a look. And a whole saddle-bag full of stuff ain't so easy to hide."

"He's a mean man to handle," I admitted, "and he's a hard one to get away from. There's no doubt about that. Still, old son, I don't quite know what brought you out here."

"It's like this," said the kid gravely. "There was Dug Waters all surrounded night and day, with the dicks watching him and every move that he made. I couldn't get to him to ask him what to do. And when I heard that Murphy was taking the trail, then I knew that I'd have to get close to somebody a little older and with more sense than me. And, of course, I thought about our partner. I thought about you, Joe. So here I am."

"Hold on," said I. "You thought about me?"

"Why, of course I did," he answered quickly.

"But look here, son," said I. "I don't have any share in deals like this. I don't work—in this line."

"Yeah, but you're a friend," said Chip.

I stared at him. I saw his meaning. A friend is a friend, no matter what the strain.

"But, suffering Moses, Chip!" said I. "Don't you realize that Tug Murphy knows that I'm a friend of yours and Waters's? Isn't he likely as not to come for me, if he hears that you've disappeared in this direction?"

Chapter Four

This idea of mine had not occurred to Chip, it appeared. He scratched his head for a time and then nodded across the dimness of the firelight.

"It was a wrong steer that I had," said he. "I ought to've remembered that the sheriff knew you were in with us in the jail break when we got Waters loose. I just forgot, kind of. I was a fool, Joe, I guess. But tomorrow I'll start along."

It made me feel sorry to see the boy repentant. That was a humor one didn't often spot in him. Generally he was fighting back if you tried to corner him.

So I said: "Look here, Chip. It's all right. Don't you worry about the thing. I'll manage it, all right. And after all, this is a tolerable big country for even the sheriff to find us in."

"Aye," said Chip, "but I've blazed the trail out here the second time. And just supposing that he should turn up!" His shoulders twitched. I saw him shudder.

"Well, it's all right," I said vaguely.

"It ain't all right," said Chip. "Because if he seen you with that saddlebag loaded with coin, what would he be thinking? Nothing at all, except that you were in on the deal."

"Oh, I can easily prove that I was out here when the robbery took place," said I.

"Yeah, but there's receivers of stolen goods, and all of that," said Chip.

"Yes," said I. "There are those, all right." I added: "You know a good deal about this stuff, it seems to me, Chip."

He sighed, and then he answered: "You know how it is, Joe. I hear a lot from Dug Waters. And I hear a lot from his pals, too."

"What pals has he got now?" I asked. "He was playing a lone hand, mostly, when I last heard about things."

"You know how it is," said Chip. "When a gent has played the game for a while, he gets sort of careless. I mean to say, he gets to thinking that he will always be able to beat it. And that's the way with Dug. He's nearly always beaten the law. And now he thinks that the law is a pup. He used never to trust nobody but me. Now he begins to trust everybody, it seems. He's softening up a good deal, I guess!"

I could have sighed, myself.

It was a wonderful thing, the way that boy had stuck to Dug Waters. They loved each other. They would have died for one another. And Dug Waters kept the hands of the kid clean all the while that he himself was going from gun fight to robbery to knife brawls. He watched out for the lad all the while, and the lad watched out for him. I was mighty fond of Dug. He was a little elegant, and had his eyebrows in the air a good part of the time, but he was the real stuff, and a friend that never forgot you. And that last thing is the most important in the world, I think.

So I stared through the dull of the firelight toward the boy, and I wondered what would come of him, and how he could possibly live that life of companionship with Waters without eventually becoming as outlawed as Waters was. Waters was having a free spell. He had been cornered. He had stood trial. And one of the smartest lawyers in the Southwest had freed him. It cost Waters a fortune, but now his record was smudged. The herring had been pulled across the trail, and he could come and go with all the other legal-minded people of the world.

It was all right for Waters. But what about the boy?

I said: "What are you going to do about settling down, Chip, one of these days?"

"Settling down?" said he.

"I mean going to school, and all that," I suggested.

"Oh, I dunno," he answered gloomily. "Don't be so dog-gone sour, Joe, will you?"

"All right," said I. "We won't talk about it."

"I think about it plenty," he went on. "But I can't cut away from Dug. He needs me. He gets pretty crazy when he's left to himself. He gets to acting like a lord, or something. He orders his ham and eggs on a gold plate, you might say. There ain't any sense in that. And Dug needs me. I sort of straighten him out. He'll listen to me— a little!"

He sighed again

"You go to bed, son," said I. "You've been up a long while, and you've had a long march."

He nodded, stood up, stretched, and rolled down his blankets. But before he turned in, dead tired as he was, he went off and found the mustang and rubbed its nose with his fist.

"Good night, you old son of a gun," said he. "I'm gonna be braining you one of these days."

Then he came back and turned in.

But I sat up a while. I was bothered by several things. One was pity for Chip, and wondering what was to come of him. One was thinking of that saddlebag loaded with a fortune. And one was of Sheriff Tug Murphy, somewhere out in the desert, most likely, and very apt to be headed my way.

Well, it was a bad business, it seemed to me. But finally I turned in myself, and lay there for a while until the stars grew misty and dull; that was the moment I went to sleep.

I woke up with something tapping the sole of my foot. I didn't open my eyes. I just said: "Don't be a dang fool, burro. Get out of here!"

He used to have a way of doing that, that fool burro I had with me. I mean, he'd come and paw at my foot, or maybe at my hand, in the middle of the night. Just for meanness, or for company; I never could make out.

That tapping at my foot kept on. So I opened my eyes and looked up to the sky, and there I saw the moon riding well above the eastern mountains, and the cold of the night air was on my face and eyes, so that I knew I had been sleeping for quite a time.

Then I looked a little lower, and I saw the sombrero and the shoulders of a man standing below me.

I didn't need another tap at my foot. I woke up pronto. And I sat up, too, and saw a burly fellow standing there with the moon over his right shoulder.

"Hello, Joe," said he.

I recognized the voice. I recognized the iron rasp in it, I mean to say. It was Sheriff Tug Murphy!

"Hello, Tug," said I. "This is a lucky kind of a surprise."

I stood up.

"Yeah, I guess it's kind of a surprise," said Tug Murphy. "Just mind your hands a little. Don't make no funny moves."

"I won't make any funny moves," said I. I added: "What's up? You're not trying to hang anything on me?"

"I dunno that I'm gonna hang anything on you," said the sheriff. "I'm just hankering after a little of your conversation."

"That's the way with bein' bright," said I to him. "People enjoy your talk so much that they just can't get along without it. They gotta ride a coupla hundred miles across the desert to hear some more of it. Sit down and rest your feet, Tug. I'll wake up the fire and get some coffee started for you."

"You just step into your boots," said Tug. "We'll let the fire and the coffee take care of itself for a while."

I dressed. And all the time I was looking out of the corner of my eye at the shine of the leather of the saddlebag that lay beside the dead embers of my fire. And in that bag there was enough to soak me into prison for ten years, I guessed.

I looked a little farther to the left toward the blankets of the kid. The blankets were there, but the kid wasn't. There was no sign of him.

He must have heard a noise and waked and got away. I took it pretty hard of him that he hadn't given me a sign, or taken away that danged saddlebag, at the least.

I dressed, as I say, and then I threw some wood onto the fire, and it began to fume and smoke. I filled the coffeepot with water out of the bucket. That water in the bucket was standing so still that a star had dropped down into it, I remember. And after the water got through slopping around, the image of the star came shuddering back again, all split and shattered into pieces. But settling down into its old self.

I was pretty thoughtful as I raked that fire together and put the pot on top of two rocks, where the flame started to lick at it and curl around it.

"A funny thing about a coffeepot," said the sheriff. "It draws the fire to it, sort of. Ever notice that?"

"Yeah," said I. "That's a funny thing, but I could tell you a lot of funnier ones."

"Like what?"

"Like you being out here," said I. "What kind of a brain storm have you got, boy?"

Tug Murphy laughed.

"You mean you're too dog-gone virtuous to be suspected, eh?" says he.

"Well, you know me, Tug," said I.

"I know you, all right," said he.

"And what have I ever pulled except a wad of tobacco out of a hip pocket?"

"That may be a true thing," says he. "I dunno. That may be a pretty true thing. But you know how it is, old son."

"What way?" said I.

"I mean, you know that rocks don't melt very easy."

"Yes," said I. "I know that pretty well."

"But still, there is fires that can melt 'em."

"Go on, Tug," said I. "I'm getting sort of tired of all this. What are you talking about, anyway?"

"I'm talking about two hundred and fifty-three thousand dollars!" says the sheriff.

I whistled. "That's enough for me," I said. "I'll take that much. But what are you driving at?"

"That money's missing from the bank," said the sheriff. "And I'm out here after it. You see that I'm playing my cards all on the table in front of you, boy?"

"Yeah, I see that," said I. "That's a compliment that you're paying to me, Tug. I've gone and wished a quarter of a million out of a bank and laid it up here. Is that it?"

I grinned across the fire at him, and he was still as serious as could be.

"I know that the kid trekked in this direction," said he. "And I know that he must have been heading for you with the cash. Now I'll tell you this. Turn over the boodle and there's not a word more said. The bank wants it too bad. Turn it over, and there'll never be a word said to you about the job, son!"

Chapter Five

It gave me a jump to hear him talk, and that I'll admit. I mean to say, there was the saddlebag, still in the corner of my eye, and if the sheriff should open it—out would come penitentiary for me. And if I turned over the stolen goods, there was an end of the trouble. I tell you that I I was tingling to tell him and just point out the saddlebag.

But then I thought of Dug Waters. He had been true blue with me. He had had my life in the palm of his hand once and he had let me go. He had saved me.

You can't forget things like that. And there were other things between us—a lot of them. It's true that I never had worked with him on any of his crooked jobs, because that's not my line. But nevertheless, there had been a good deal between us, and I was mighty fond of Waters. There was the kid, too. What would Chip do if I let the saddlebag slip through my fingers into the hands of the law? He would never forgive me, and that was plain!

Well, during about a tenth part of a second I thoroughly sifted every one of these questions, and then I decided that, law or no law, danger or no danger, friends came first, and I couldn't blab.

"Tug," said I, "it's a sort of inspiring thing to hear you ask me for a quarter of a million. It shows the kind of faith that you have in me. There may be a quarter of a million in these mountains, but my luck is so bad that it would take me a thousand years to get it. Right now

I'm taking about four or five dollars a day out of this here ground, and breaking my back, at that."

When he heard this he laughed a little.

"You know what I mean, old son," said he. "I'm talking about cash from a bank. And the kid must have brought it here."

"You mean Chip?"

"Who else would I mean?" said he.

The coffee was beginning to simmer and to throw up the nose of its steam straight out of the spout, and the fragrance spread around over the place and smelled pretty good.

"Chip's not been here," said I.

He lurched his shoulders forward and stuck out his jaw. "He's not been here?" he echoed.

"No," said I, as steadily as I could. "He's not been here."

And I looked straight back across the fire into the eyes of the sheriff.

I could see the savage twist of his lips and the evil in his eyes. A mean man was Tug Murphy when his blood was up, and it didn't take much to get it up.

"Have a can of coffee," said I. "There's no poison in it. Here's some sugar, too." I handed the things over.

He stirred in the sugar, still staring at me as though he could eat me.

"What you doin' with sugar this long out?" said he. "How come it lasted so long?"

"You know," said I, "that I've always had a sort of sweet tooth. So I take along a good supply. But the fact is that this isn't my sugar."

"No," said he, "I'll bet that it's not your sugar. It's the stuff that Chip brought."

"Chip?" said I. "You've got Chip on the brain."

"I got reason to have him on the brain," said he. "He's laid me the trickiest trail that I've ever followed—and I've rode after Indians, son!"

"Yeah, Chip could lay you a hard trail to follow," I agreed. "But I guess you won't find him here, Tug."

He shrugged his heavy shoulders. The coffee was very hot, so he sipped it noisily. And then, breathing up it, he sipped it again. He was not a pretty man to watch, I can tell you, and he was staring at me as though I were red meat.

"Old son Joe," said he, "I reckon that you're lyin' to me."

"All right," said I. "You go on reckonin'. And the real crook will be getting miles away from you."

He only grinned. "You out here all alone?" he said.

"Me?" said I.

"Yeah. They told me back yonder that you'd come out all alone."

I remembered the rumpled blankets of the kid, and I answered:

"No, I'm not alone. I was alone when I started, but I'm not alone now. A funny thing happened. You know old Chris Winter?"

"Yeah. I know old Chris," said he. "I used to, anyway."

"Well," said I, "old Chris, he got it into his head that he'd strike out in this direction, and when he heard where I intended to prospect, he came along and found me, and we teamed up. It's pretty good to have somebody to talk to, you know, even if it's no more than old Chris."

"Sour old sinner, ain't he?" said the sheriff.

"Yeah. He's sort of sour, but he's all right," said I.

"Where is he now?" asked the sheriff. "Does he smell sheriffs a long distance off and get restless and go walking?"

"You know how it is," said I. "He's got insomnia."

"No, I don't know how it is," said he. "He's got 'in' what?"

" 'Somnia," said I. "He can't sleep very good."

"Can't he?" said the sheriff. "Maybe he ain't got the words, but he certainly can play the tune. I recollect makin' a trip through Inyo County in California, and old Chris Winter was along, and dog-gone his heart if he didn't make the mountains tremble all night long, he snored so loud! I never heard such snorin'."

"It must've busted down his nerves," I suggested. "Anyway, he's a pretty light sleeper now."

"Dog-gone me, but I'm glad to hear it," said Tug Murphy.

"So he gets up," said I, "and he goes off for a walk in the middle of the night when he finds out he can't sleep.

It's hard lines on the old feller, all right. But he don't whimper much."

"How long has he been out here with you?" says the sheriff.

"Quite a spell," says I. "Let's see: yeah—it's quite a while, now, that the old boy has been out here with me."

"That's a mighty interesting thing," said the sheriff. "Does he look kind of nacheral, too?"

"Why, sure he does," said I. "That face of his couldn't look anyway but natural. It would break, otherwise."

I thought this was a pretty good joke, so I laughed a little, but I couldn't help noticing that the sheriff did not seem to be in the least amused.

Then he says: "There's a lot of interest in this for me. I've always been pretty interested in ghosts and spirits and things."

"What do you mean?" says I.

"Why, man," says he, "ain't Chris been dead for three months and more?"

It was a hard jolt for me. It was a punch on the point of the chin, so to speak. I got my breath and my wits back as well as I could.

The sheriff went on: "Chris was workin' on the Morgan and Rister crew, and he goes and falls down a shaft. Now, wasn't that a fool thing for an old hand like him to do? But I'm glad to see that his ghost has come out here to carry on with the drill. He was always a wonderful good hand with a single jack, was Chris Winter."

I let the sheriff carry along. I was trying to think. But I couldn't make much progress. He was grinning and chuckling all the while.

"Well, Tug," I said at last, "the fellow who's out here as my partner is not Chris Winter. Though I wish that name had gone down. He is a light sleeper, though, and he don't want to see you."

"I'll bet he don't," said the sheriff. "In a word, you might as well admit that it's the kid."

I shook my head. I grinned at the sheriff. I poured out another can of coffee for him; but all the while he was studying me with a lowering look, and presently he said:

"You know, Joe, that you're stepping pretty deep into this business. I don't want to do you no harm. So far as I know, you've always been straight. But if I have to take you back to town with me, they'll slam you into the pen for a pretty long term. The judges and the juries around here in Nevada are getting pretty mean. You gotta fish and drag about fifty or a hundred square mile to get yourself a jury, in the first place; and all that riding the jurymen have got to do, day after day, it riles them a lot. They vote you guilty because they're saddle-sore! Now, Joe, you straighten up and tell me the truth, and it'll be all right. But if you don't, I start trouble right pronto."

I admired to hear the way that the sheriff put the case. It showed that he was a pretty straight fellow, at heart. I liked Tug Murphy before. I liked him better than ever, now.

But what could I do?

I already had thought the thing back and forth. He had proved me a liar, on the jump, and now what was I to do?

Well, finally I shook my head. I said:

"Tug, suppose that everything you think were true— which it isn't—still, I wouldn't help you any. You ought to know that I couldn't."

"Because the kid's your friend, and Waters is your friend," said he.

"Put it any way you like," said I.

"Then—stick your hands out!" says he.

He took out a pair of handcuffs and held them on his left hand.

"Aw, come along, Tug," said I. "D'you think that I'm going to try any gun play?"

"I don't like to put irons on you, Joe," said he. "I've seen you to be too dang decent for that. I don't want to do it. Will you give me your word that you'll sit tight and make no move while I take a look around this here camp?"

"Well, I'll do that," said I.

"Not make no move at all?" he insisted.

"No, I'll sit tight," said I.

He hesitated, and then he nodded. He dropped the things back into his pocket, and I was glad to see them go. Then he stood up and looked around the camp. There was not much to it, I know, but the mischief told him where to go. He walked out, first, and found the mule, and rubbed his hand along the side of it.

"The pack saddle come off this mule no later than tonight, Joe," said he. "I can tell by the salt that ain't rubbed out of the hair yet."

I said nothing, because there was really nothing to say. I felt like a fool because I hadn't rubbed the mule and the bronco down.

Then Tug came back toward the fire, stubbed his toe against the saddlebag—and opened it up!

He just pulled one handful out of that bag and stood there looking not at what he held, but across the fire, toward my face.

Chapter Six

Well, to make a pretty long story short, we started on the march for jail. We only waited for the morning, and then we lighted out together. The sheriff had come out with a change of horses. He had two good, tough mustangs, rather lumpy in the heads, and with hips like the hips of cows. But they could keep going through fire. And that's the sort of horse one wants for riding through Nevada.

Tug Murphy was pretty decent to me. He just arranged a rope that run from one of my wrists to the other, and left about a foot of play between my hands. That way, I could make a smoke, light a match, and even do my share of work around camp when he halted. It was only, as you might say, a short hobble for my hands. The sheriff apologized for it. I'll never forget his apology. He said:

"Look here, Joe. I could take you in with irons on, which would make you feel like a dog. Or else I could put nothing on you at all. But that would mean taking your word for honor first that you wouldn't escape. And I've got no right to take your word on that. If you have a right good chance to bust me over the head and make away, you go ahead and do it. It's your right. Because, as sure as tarnation, I'm takin' you in for a long stretch up the river. But now I've got the rope on you, it makes me easier; it makes you more comfortable; and it's better all around.

Only, it makes me feel pretty mean to rope a man like a calf. And a he-man, and a real man, like you, Joe!"

I appreciated that compliment, coming from the sheriff. He didn't drop many like it in his conversation, you may be sure!

Well, of course I couldn't blame the sheriff. I only wondered what the deuce would become of me, and now and then, inside my mind, I certainly danged that boy Chip. For he had known that the sheriff was on his trail, and yet he had led right out to me. Well, now the thing was ended, and I was due for prison, and I groaned as I thought about it.

What shall I say about that inland voyage? I'll only say this, that all the beauty went out of Nevada, as I rode along. All the beauty went out, and the ugliness came in.

The blue went out of the sky and the color went out of the distances.

For one thing, just as we started, the Old Nick stoked up in his furnace and turned on an extra blast. Perhaps I was not so used to the heat of the valleys, I had been working such a height up the side of the mountain; but when we dropped into the bottom, it was like dropping into a white road. The glare shot up through the eyes and came out at the top of the head.

I knocked along pretty much like a mule, with my head down. Sometimes a hot wind came shooting at us and the mustangs put their heads down and just shuddered and endured it. But they could not take a step until that wind had gone by, in a whoop. One of those blasts would take every drop of moisture out of the clothes and off the face, and just leave salt traces where the perspiration had been. When the horses were dripping with moisture, they would be wiped dry in ten seconds, and the salt lay all over their hides in little lines, like those the waves leave on the shore.

I've seen it hot in other places. Perhaps humid heat is worse. But I've never hankered after living on the hot side of an oven, and that was what we were riding through.

The sheriff didn't mind it so much.

I wouldn't have minded, either, if I'd been in his boots. He was pretty sure to get at least a ten-thousand-dollar reward from the bank, unless the bank was a set of pikers. Besides, there was the fame.

Tug used to talk over the possibilities of what he would get. It was his favorite theme all the way we rode together.

The first night we camped out in the naked flat, a dry camp. Tug wanted to shoot the burro and the mule. He said that he would charge the expenses off to his personal account. But I wouldn't let him shoot the burro. That mean little beast had been company for me too long up there by the mine. It had seen me through some lovely spots, and I liked the cock of its long, wise ears. That burro could carry his own weight on a cupful of water and a ham sandwich, so to speak. I've heard the camel praised for powers of endurance, but the camel is a regular parlor exhibit compared with a real, hundred-per-cent Mexican burro. As for the mule, that belonged to Chip. I couldn't tell the sheriff that—no matter how sure he was—but I gathered that it wouldn't be a good idea to put a bullet through anything that belonged to that boy. I said so, and the sheriff saw the light.

"He's Irish," said the sheriff. "He's Irish, like me. And you never can tell where an Irishman will put his heart. Might put his heart on a woman, a horse, or a stone. But when he does, that woman, that horse, and that stone he's ready to die for. No, I guess that I'd better not shoot the mule. It might be Chip's favorite."

It was a strange speech to listen to, that.

So we slogged along right out into the flat middle of the desert. That was not a dry camp, thank goodness. There was a little pool of alkali water. It was scummed around the edges, and it was bitter as aloes. But it tasted good enough when it was made into coffee. We drank our coffee, and ate our flapjacks and bacon, and felt the heat still rising from the ground like steam.

Great Scott, how hot it was!

Then the night breeze wakened and came softly about us, flowing like water, and we took off our clothes mostly, and let it blow. And while we were lying there in the blankets, for a while, cooling and trying to forget that the next day's march would be a lot worse than this one, the sheriff said:

"We'll have decent water, at the end of that march. I know where the pool is. It's fenced all around with rocks. It comes up and starts to flowing, and it goes about twenty feet and then goes down under the sand again. But it flows

112

enough to keep it sweet, and it's cool, too, and there's a couple of specks of blue that fall into it out of the sky; but all the rest of the face of it is kept dark by the shadow of the rocks. It's the kind of a water hole that a man could dream about."

"Shut up, Tug," said I. "I'm dreamin' about it already. I'm thinkin' how it will wash the road down my throat. That's what I'm thinkin' about. And the alkali—there ain't any alkali in it, you say?"

"It's as sweet," said Tug, after a moment, "as heaven! As sweet as heaven with stars in it. And that's what I mean! It's a dog-gone honest spring, that's what it is!"

All at once, I felt the whole lining of my throat go dry and crack with yearning, but I didn't get up to take a drink from our pool of this evening. I knew a little too much for that. The more you drink of alkali water, the worse off you are, and all the sicker. It only keeps you from dying of thirst, and that's all.

Says the sheriff: "Maybe they'll make it twenty-five."

I knew that he was thinking about how big his reward would be. I said nothing. Just then, the mule gives a snort, and then starts into a loud braying.

"What's the matter with that fool mule?" said the sheriff, and sits up. "What's it seen?"

"Nothing," said I. "You know the way it is with a mule, Tug. You know why it starts in to braying, once in a while, like it was crying for help?"

"Yeah. I know what you mean," said he. "You tell me why?"

"Sure," said I. "It's because even a mule gets so dog-gone tired of its own mean nature that it wants a change. And when you hear a mule bawling like that, it's just up and asking heaven for a second chance."

Tug Murphy lay back again onto his blankets, slowly.

"Maybe you're right," says he. "I never knew a mule very well without beginning to pity it, finally. They're just sons of torment, Joe."

"They are," said I. "And that reminds me of a story about the—"

"They might even make it thirty," says the sheriff.

I saw that he was back on the question of the reward, again. I said nothing. I'd heard enough on that subject.

"But then again," said the sheriff, "you take a mean

113

man like President Ranger of that bank, and he's as likely as not to say that I done no more than what I was paid by the county for doing."

This time I put in my word.

"Yeah, as likely as not," said I.

The sheriff grunted.

"It's a cool quarter of a million," said he. "They oughta by rights pay me ten per cent, if they got any heart."

"Ah-hunh," says I.

"And even if they make it only five per cent, that's twelve thousand five hundred."

"Uh-hunh," says I.

"But they wouldn't be short sports. They'd have to make it a round figure. Say, fifteen thousand."

"Or ten," says I.

"Yeah. Or even cut it down as far as ten," says the sheriff. "You talk like a regular banker, Joe. I bet you'd do fine behind the rails of a bank, collecting interest, and things."

"Uh-hunh," says I.

"Well, that ought to be rock bottom," says the sheriff. "And on ten thousand, a man could do a lot. There's Pig Weller has set himself up with a pretty good layout, all that a man would ask to have; and his whole outfit, land, and stock, and all, it only set him back eight thousand."

"He didn't get much stock for that," says I.

"No, but he part paid on 'em, and they'll turn into hard cash for him."

"Uh-hunh," says I.

"The old woman, she'd like to settle down," says he.

Then he sat up again.

"What's the matter?" says I.

"That fool of a mule," says he, "where's it walking to? And it's got the horses right along after it."

"Well, maybe it smells good grass," said I.

"They're stepping right out," says he. "And yet I hobbled 'em pretty short. They're stepping right out, for hobbled stock—"

Suddenly he jumped up to his feet.

"By the eternal nation," he says, soft as you please, so that it sent a chill down my spine, "them hobbles have been cut!"

That got me to my feet, too, and I was in time to see

114

some figure—it looked small—jump on the back of the sheriff's best mustang and start off at a trot, and then at a canter, with all the rest of the live stock on lead ropes behind, and the burro last of all pulling back hard on its line!

Chapter Seven

I heard the sheriff groan. Then he grabbed his rifle and started pumping bullets at the disappearing caravan of horses, and mules, and what not.

But he had no luck. You could tell beforehand that he would have no luck. The cause being that moonlight is the worst light in the world for shooting. Everything seems clear, but at a little distance, and no one in the world can judge the distances.

I knew that he would miss, and he did miss.

And I saw our transportation wander off into the distance.

"Indians!" I yelled. "And this is why people that steal horses are hanged."

"Indians your foot," said the sheriff, strangely calm. "It's Chip. That's what it is."

"Chip?" I shouted. "Chip leave me stranded like this? Never in a thousand years!"

"Who does he like better?" said the sheriff. "You or Waters?"

"He may like Waters better," said I, "but he'd never do a trick like this to me—not in the middle of the desert!"

"You don't know him," said the sheriff. "But I do. Because he's Irish, and the Irish blood is all red and black. There ain't any blue in it. I'm Irish, too. But we'll win through to Freshwater Springs!"

You can imagine that we didn't wait. If we had to hoof it through those shifting sands, that slid back six inches under every step, there was no sense in waiting for the sun to come up and broil us. It was better to start tired than to start hot.

We sifted down our packs to almost nothing. We just kept one rifle, some food, and the saddlebag that had the quarter of a million dollars. Then we started across the gloom and silver of the moonlit desert.

I can't tell you how the loss of our horses had widened that desert. The place had seemed big enough, before, but now it seemed a lot bigger. I can tell you. It was multiplied by ten.

Off we went, and I listened to the sand gritting and sliding under my feet, and I listened to the sand gritting and sliding under the feet of the sheriff.

He was very calm about it. Now and then he would break out into a short speech, but mostly he saved his breath.

"About fifteen years in jail," he said several times. "That's about all that he'll get. And I hope that they make him perspire from morning to night for fifteen years, the way that I'm doing now. I hope that they keep the whip on him. Dog-gone his miserable hide!"

I nodded.

I was very fond of Chip, but if he really were guilty of this business I hoped that he would get plenty of punishment, and not have to wait for a future life to receive it, either.

Well, we slogged along. I don't know how many of you have walked across blow sand. I hope for your own sakes that not many have. It's lighter than water and a good deal more slippery. There's no way of planting your feet that gives a good purchase. The best way is to turn your toes out and your foot on a bias. That way, you get more to push against. Well, even at the best it's a bad business. It's wading, and slipping, and sliding. Every pound that you carry counts for ten, in blow sand.

Pretty soon, we talked no more, but just buckled down, and laid into the work, and set our teeth, and hoped that Chip, or the Indian or whoever had stolen our horses, might land in the hot place.

Then the sun came up.

It didn't waste any time warming up. It just slugged us in the head with about ninety degrees for a beginning. The instant that it got its eye above the horizon mist, it was blazing hot, and it kept right on blazing. You have no idea how the desert sun starts its business with the first

116

signal and keeps right on until it sinks. It shoots from the hip, without a waste motion, and it keeps on shooting, all day long.

Our canteens lasted until the middle of the morning. Then we made a halt in the lee side of some rocks, and the sheriff swallowed a couple of times to ease his throat, and he said:

"Well, we'll make the Freshwater Springs, all right. But it's going to be tough."

He was right.

He generally was right, but particularly about this. We slogged along through that blow sand with the sun getting hotter and hotter. It seared through a man's shirt and burned the shoulders. It blistered the rims of the ears. It scorched the end of the nose. Now and then I raised my heavy, broad-brimmed sombrero, and tried to get some air on my head in that way. But it was no good. It let the steam off, so to speak, but it didn't let any air in.

Well, I went along and endured it. Once you've got used to desert travel, you can remember other times when it seemed eternal, and yet it ended, some time.

But the worst part about the Nevada deserts is that there's often a blue pile of mountains off somewhere on the rim of the horizon telling you about cold running water, and shade under trees, and winds blowing, and all such things.

I dreamed of palaces of ice. And I could have eaten the whole dog-gone palace!

Then we hove over a rise, and the sheriff laughed in a horrible, soundless way, and he pointed and said:

"There's the Freshwater Springs. Down there, where the rocks are shining!"

Well, suddenly my feet were light, and my heart was light, and I stepped along free and gay and bold and could almost have sung, except that my throat was hurting me too badly.

We stepped along pretty briskly on that stretch, and then as we came closer to the rocks, the sheriff he gives a queer, choked yell, and then he breaks into a run.

I watched him. I thought that the heat and the thirst had driven him a little crazy.

But then I saw something that made me start running, also. For those rocks didn't look the way rocks should look. They seemed to have been turned every which way, and their pale bellies were turned to the sun.

I ran as hard as I could, but I couldn't keep up with the sheriff. He was a heavy-built man, but that day he fairly had the foot of me; and when I came up, puffing, and groaning, he was standing with both hands spread out, as though he were making an explanation, silently, to some one who could understand silence.

Then I saw for myself.

Freshwater Springs had been blown up!

Yes, there were the rocks, as I have said, scattered about, and now one could see how they were scorched and blackened, here and there. But the main thing was that the water was gone—all gone!

The rim markings of the pool were there. The sand was still almost damp enough to chew, if you know what I mean. But the water was gone.

Some fiend had dropped a charge away down the throat of the springs and had blown it, and the flow of the water had been stopped.

What could one do? Well, the next prospector who happened along might drop down another charge of powder and blow it again, and then the water would likely start running. But now it was lost.

And we had no powder!

I looked at the sheriff, and the sheriff, he looked back at me. He grinned, and his smile was a bad thing to see.

"Chip!" said he.

"Not Chip," said I. "Chip would never do such a thing. Not Chip! Chip's a partner of mine."

Said the sheriff: "Am I Irish?"

"Yes," said I.

"Do I know the Irish?" said he.

"You ought to," I admitted.

"Did I say that Irish blood was all red and black?" he asked me fiercely.

"You said that."

"And no blue in it?"

"No," said I.

"That's Chip," said the sheriff. "He's all red and black. The red in him is the way that he loves his friend, Waters. And the black is the way that he feels about everybody else."

118

I shook my head. "He's only a kid," said I. "He couldn't do it. He couldn't have the heart in him to do it."

"Aye, he could," said the sheriff. "He's got an Irish heart!"

I listened to him talking, and it seemed to me that there must be some other answer, but still my mind turned back again and again to the same thought. It was Chip. He had the reason to want to plague the sheriff, and if he plagued me at the same time—well, what difference did it make?

Anger came into me like steel, and I gritted my teeth, and wished that I had the neck of that boy in my hands. I would give it a twisting that would end Chip's days of mischief.

"Chip done it," said the sheriff, over and over. "Chip went and done it. He never stopped to reckon the time when I was pretty easy on him. I mean the time that I pinched Waters and could've pinched Chip, too. But I didn't. I didn't want to send an Irish spark like that to the penitentiary. Well, this is the way that he pays me back."

It was an interesting thing to hear the sheriff talk like that, slowly, quietly, with a voice rusted and grating with emotion, and thirst. I listened to him, and I watched the bulldog working in his face, and I almost forgot my own thirst, I was so keen to see what was in the sheriff's mind.

Well, after a time we thought the thing over, and we talked it over in just a few words, because not many words were necessary. The nature of the deed stood up and looked us in the face.

We had to get from Freshwater Springs—the very name was a torture, now—to the next water hole. And that water hole was a good seventy miles away.

Seventy miles, and sand to trudge through! Seventy miles! We would have to go slogging all through this day, and all the night we would have to keep marching, and most of the following day. And, at the end of our march, we'd come to a few swallows of muddy alkali water, if we were lucky.

I wanted to lick my lips, but I didn't. I just pressed them in a little, and made the saliva flow a bit.

We sat there in the scanty shadow of one of the overturned rocks, and we decided what direction we would have to take. I knew that country pretty well, and we picked out the valley where I knew of a water hole that was said never to go dry—perhaps.

Then we got up and buried the saddlebag, and started off.

Chapter Eight

When I put the saddlebag in so casually, I meant it.

It didn't matter to the sheriff, either. All that mattered to us was seventy miles of desert sand—and how were we going to last out? We both had been through the grind before. We knew the desert. We weren't romantic about it. But a few touches of that dry, hot wind would simply soak up the blood from our bodies; and we'd die.

It wasn't so much body, either. It was mind that the heat worked on. It was well enough for the sun to scorch the body, but it was a different thing to let the thought of it start to campaigning in the brain. That was what drove men crazy.

So you can believe me when I say that we put away a quarter of a million dollars under the broken rocks of Freshwater Springs and gave it not a thought. And we marched on without once looking back. The rifle was there with the saddlebag, too. We had no use for that weight. We carried with us some salt, and a little jerked beef; and the sheriff kept his hunting knife on, not that he wanted it, I dare say, but because he would have felt undressed and strange without its handle to fumble as we went along.

Two hundred and fifty thousand dollars lay there under the rocks, and we would have changed the whole sum, believe me, for a single runt of a mustang to ride by turns, and to hang onto, to help us forward over the terrible stretch that lay ahead.

We had only one thing to be glad of, and that was that we had company. I think, for my part, that if I had been alone I would simply have stretched out there in the shade of the rocks and waited for death. Or perhaps I could have helped it on the way a little. But with a companion, a man

120

doesn't give in. The last thing that remains to us, it appears, is pride and a sense of audience. The sheriff was my audience. I was his audience. And so we just headed away for the cleft in the distant mountains where I knew that water could be found.

I think that the most awful part of it was the knowledge that the hours would crawl away before us like a worm, and that always we would be looking at that picture of blue distance, and that always we would seem to be as far away as ever, and that even when the picture turned from blue to brown, we would still have a ghastly march ahead of us, and that even when we could see individual rocks and trees, still there would remain terrible miles before us.

The clear air would take care of that.

Yes, the moment would come when we would suck our own blood to ease the horrible pain in our cracking throats.

And we both knew all these things. And we both knew that it was touch and go for us. That was the reason that we wasted no breath in talk.

The sheriff simply cut the cord that tied my hands. And I felt no particular gratitude for the act. It might be I who would hang onto reason the longest and be able to slap him on the back at the right moment, and clear his own wits, or curse him into a greater manhood.

On the other hand, it might be he.

So we left the rocks, and we started our voyage, and we walked all the rest of that day.

I don't want to dwell on it. I don't want to recall the horror of that sun, or the way it laid its red-hot hand against the backs of our heads and fried the brains. I don't want to think of that day, because it makes my throat dry and crack—the mere thought. Now I can go and fill a glass with ice and pour in enough water to fill the interstices, and drink that water, and fill up the ice again, and sip once more, and let the blessed cold of it trickle slowly down my throat. But still it seems that the thirst can never be taken out of me. The water famine has its claws in my vitals once more, and I burn with it, in imagination, almost as badly as I burned on that day.

Before night came, I knew that we couldn't succeed.

Already my tongue was badly swollen, and my lips were cracking till the blood ran down my chin. It was a painful thing to have to move my eyes, because the balls of them seemed to be lined and set in sharp crystals of quartz.

But we marched on.

The sheriff must have known we were beaten, too. His case was worse than mine, because he was a larger and a grosser man, and I could tell by his staring look, long before sundown, that he was looking his death in the face. But, you see, he would not be the first to weaken, and neither would I.

There was the strange picture of two men walking straight on toward inevitable death and never speaking about it, because each of us wished to break down the pride of the other and force him to be the first to whine. Twenty times complaints came pouring up into my throat and twenty times I ate those complaints and said no word of them. And once—once only—I heard the sheriff curse, and his curse was a groan.

Now, it was about the sunset time, when the next part of that adventure started. I mean to say, the sun was lying on its side in the west as hot and terrible as ever, nearly, but its cheeks were swelling, and it was plain that before long we would have the dark. And even that thought was no comfort because, some time during the dark of that night, the knees would fail under one of us, and that man would sink, and the other would turn and give him one look, and then drop in turn because of the bitter comfort of dying beside a friend.

But, as this sunset began, and the sky was starting to redden in the west, I saw the sheriff pause sharply and stretch out his arm.

"It's begun," I said to myself. "The madness is at him, and eating his brain like a mouse nibbling at cheese. It's started on him, and he'll be raving, in another moment."

But he stood there like a statute, just pointing, and saying nothing until I turned my eyes with pain in the same direction.

Then I saw it.

Animals of some sort were coming toward us, strung out in a long string, etched strongly against the background of the western light, and dyed and blackened by the contrast. And while I watched them, and saw the nodding heads of the horses, I groaned aloud with joy.

They were not wild horses. No, now I could see a rider

122

upon the first of the lot, and I thought that that must be the luckiest man in the entire universe, because he was in this desert, but he had a horse beneath him.

Suppose he were thirsty. Suppose he ran out of water. Suppose he had to drink. Then he could cut the throat of one of his lead animals—mules or horses—and he could drink the blood. And what a delicious drink that seemed to me, at the time!

The sheriff dropped his arm.

"Chip!" said he.

It rather staggered me, that idea. I stared again—one small rider, with several horses or mules behind—yes, and at the tail of all, the little outline of the burro, pressed against the ground, as it were.

"It's Chip," I yelled, as though I had made the discovery first.

The sheriff grinned, and as he smiled, the blood ran down his face from his broken lips.

But he nodded, and side by side, we turned toward that procession. It was Chip, and after all, he cared for us enough to want to give us a hand.

We marched toward him. The sun sank in the west. All was red fire behind, when we came within shouting distance of that youngster. And we saw him wave an arm to make us halt.

We walked straight on. The wave of an arm could not stop us. Suddenly something struck the sand at my feet, and a shower of that sand was scattered over my legs. Then the clang of a rifle dinted on my ears.

He was shooting to make us halt!

Well, bullets have a persuasive power of their own, and we stood still.

Then I heard Chip's voice, not raised and strained but easy and cool as you please.

"You want water, you fellows?"

Want water? The very sound of the word worked at my saliva glands and made my throat crack again, and widen in hope.

We merely stood still and waved at him, like fools. But we had no voice to carry across that distance.

"I've got plenty of water here for you," came the voice of Chip again, "but before you get it, you make a bargain with me."

123

He paused. We both waved. What was the use of words? Of course, he could make his bargain on his own terms. If he had water, he was the king of the world, so far as we were concerned.

Then came the thin crowing of his voice again:

"I've picked up the whole show that you left behind you. I've picked up the saddlebag, and all your packs. I've got the money. And I want to know if I keep it easy and safe, or do I ride on and let you sizzle and stew here?"

Do you see the idea? He would offer us rescue, but he would only do so under the condition that we should agree not to touch him and the possessions which he had taken.

I began to laugh, the laughter sounding like a whisper. Heaven, how my throat hurt!

Then I looked at the sheriff and saw that he was shaking his head from side to side with a long, slow swing, the way a bullock does, if you've ever seen one under a yoke.

I was amazed, and I stared at him again. Refusing? Saying no to this offer of water—of life! By heaven, that was what he was doing! He was saying no!

He put out his hand and gave my arm a grip.

"You go on," says this amazing sheriff. "You go on and get the water. But me—you know the way it is."

"I know that you're crazy in the head," said I. "That's what I know. I don't know how else it is. What do you mean when you ask me if I know how it is?"

I shook him. He kept on swaying his head from side to side, saying "No," not to me but to something in himself. Yes, saying "No" to the infernal heat and wretchedness of thirst that was in him.

"You know how it is," said the croaking voice of the sheriff. "I wouldn't mind giving in. But I took a dog-gone oath when I took my office. You know how it is, Joe. I swore that I'd serve the people to the best of my ability. That means what? That means with my life, if I got to. That's what it means now. You go on and get your drink. Get it good and deep. You go on, and you forget about me. I've got my job to do."

No, it was not craziness. It was greatness. That big rough-neck of a sheriff, he was great. It hit me between the eyes.

And, while I stood there gaping, almost forgetting my

thirst, by thunder, Tug Murphy turned around and marched away with a good, long, swinging step, putting distance with his last strength between himself and temptation!

Chapter Nine

Well, I was no sheriff, and I had taken no oath. But all at once I wanted to read one of those oaths that public men take before they get into office. I think, with most of them, that what they swear to do doesn't ride them very hard. No, I think that they take it pretty easy. They just have the words read off to them by a judge, or something, and they put their fat, pink hands on a book, and they say "I do," and that's all there is to it.

But Tug Murphy was different.

I could somehow see him with his head canted over to one side, listening, and nodding, and frowning, as he listened to the reading. I could see him go and take the book out of the hand of the judge and then follow the words for himself, underlining them with one blunt forefinger, with a cracked and black and broken finger nail. He wasn't a pretty man, Tug Murphy. But he was a great man. Just then it seemed to me that he made everything else shrink—even the desert, even the thirst of it.

However, what tied him did not tie me.

I went straight on toward Chip, and I went at a run, stumbling a little, my knees pretty loose.

When I got there, Chip was off his horse and waiting for me. He had a canteen that was wrapped up in a sacking, and he had so much water that he had been able to afford to use some of it to wet the sacking, and the evaporation had kept that water cool.

He shoved that canteen at me, and I grabbed it.

I didn't just swig it down. No, sir, I sat on the sand, and Chip, he kneeled behind me and made a brace for my back. He kept saying:

"Joe, old partner, you'll never forgive me. Heaven'll

125

never forgive me for what I've done to you. And Dug Waters, he'll give me what for. He'll give me a regular lambasting. But somehow, I didn't know what else to do. And I been suffering for you, Joe. And I've kept this here water cool for you, as good as I could. D'you think that you could ever forgive me, Joe?"

I hardly heard him. The words he spoke sounded far off and dim as the sunset on the borders of my mind. What mattered to me was that canteen which was shaking in my hands, and the tin lip of it rattling against my teeth.

I didn't pour it down.

No, no! A thirst like that was a treasure, and I intended to use up every penny of it. So first I let a thin trickle flow over my broken, dead lips. And some of that water ran down my chin and dropped onto my chest. And I took the canteen away from my lips before I ever had swallowed a drop, and I just sat there, leaning back against the knees of Chip, and I let that water soak through to the skin, and then I laughed a little, in spite of the hurt of laughter, to think that my skin was drinking before my throat had tasted a drop.

Yes, I laughed a little, and Chip, he grabbed me hard and said:

"Steady there, Joe. Steady, partner. Don't you let yourself go! Don't you let yourself go—"

And he began to blubber a little.

I mean, Chip was about as hard as they make them. Rawhide and whalebone was what he was made of. But still, he began to cry a little, through his teeth, fighting it down—crying in a high whine, because he thought that my brain was gone, and that the long drought had about finished me.

But my brain wasn't gone. No, no, I was only thinking the thing out—and laughing because the water had touched my body before it touched my throat.

Then I raised the canteen again, and Chip put around one brown dirty hand and steadied it for me, and this time I let a thin trickle go floating right straight down my throat.

Down my throat? I tell you, it percolated all through me, and I could feel it work. The strongest redeye in the world never worked as sure and steady and straight as that water did, soaking around through my veins and telling me what life was all about.

I don't want to exaggerate, but while I sat there and slowly sipped that canteen full of water, it seemed to me that the desert had changed, and that the green grass was pushing up all around us, and that trees were putting down root and lifting their heads. And it was pretty good to me, I tell you, to sit there and think of all that, and feel that I was in the middle of a land drenched with water to the core, and ripe and rich and flowing with green.

Perhaps I was a little twisted in the mind, after all. I don't know. I only know that before that canteen was gone, my head seemed to clear, and I sat up and made myself a cigarette, and Chip lighted it for me, and I began to smoke. And I laughed as I smoked, because I thought of what a torture smoke would have been to me ten minutes before this!

No, I sat there and smoked, and put a hand on my knee, and wondered why it was shaking so badly.

Then I felt a tapping at my shoulder, and a voice tapping at my ear.

Pretty soon the voice got in to where I could understand what it was saying:

"What's the matter with poor old Tug Murphy? What's the matter with him? Is he dippy? Why didn't he come in with you? Shall I go and get him now? Is it all right for me to leave you now and go and get him, Joe?"

Gradually, I realized everything all over again. I shook my head.

"It's not all right. It's not safe for you," said I. "He's sworn his oath that he'll serve the people. And he won't go back on the oath. He knows that you've got the money. He came out to get it. And now that he can't get it, he'll go and die. That's all there is to it. If you go near him, he'll grab you."

Chip groaned. It was like the groan of a man. His heart was all in it.

"Now I know what Waters meant!" said he.

"Waters meant what?" said I. "What did Waters say?"

"That Murphy was kind of stupid, but that he was a great man, all right."

"Aye," said I. "He's a great man. I never saw a greater. He makes me feel like a puling baby."

"What're we gunna do?" asks Chip.

127

"We're just gunna think," said I. "We're gunna think it over and see what to do. Where away is the sheriff now?"

"You can see the head and shoulders of him, marching off there," said Chip, pointing.

"Aye," said I. "He's thinking of his death. Every step he's taking is deeper into the ground, Chip."

The kid began to blubber again. He wrung his hands.

"I dunno what to do," said he. "I meant it right. It took me time to get up to Freshwater Springs after I'd blown it, and after you came. It took me a lot of time. And then one of the mustangs threw half a shoe, and I had to wrestle with the part that was left, to get it off. And that was why I didn't come up to you quicker, Joe. I never meant that you should have to march half a day, thinking of water all the way."

"It's done," said I. "It's over with."

But I was wrong. It wasn't over with. No, sir, the ache, and the misery, and the burn of it, still come back to me, and they always will, and make a groaning in my throat that sometimes wakes me up at night. However, I could understand what had been the way with Chip. He was playing his game against two grown men, and part of the time those two grown men had a rifle.

There was a little nick in Chip's left ear. It was a fresh cut. And it was clipped out by one of the sheriff's rifle bullets. After all, he had been able to shoot pretty well, even by moonlight, and that was how close Chip had come to paying for his trick with his life.

"The sheriff—" Chip kept saying. "What'll I do? If you take him water and a horse, he'll light out after me, and he'll likely catch me. Because I'm mighty tired, Joe. Jiminy, I never seem to've known what being tired was like before!" And he shook his head and sighed.

I nodded. It wasn't easy.

"You could cache the saddlebag somewhere. Then it wouldn't matter if he caught you," said I.

"I couldn't do that," said Chip. "The saddlebag ain't mine. It's Waters's. It belongs to him, and he left it in my keeping. I don't dare to let it go."

"Then what'll we do for the sheriff?" said I. "He's got to have water, and food, and a horse, or he'll never pull through. Because he's on his last legs!"

There was a little silence between us.

Then Chip said:

"My Jiminy, I wish that he was a Chinaman, or something. Then I wouldn't care. But he ain't. He's a man. Even Dug Waters ain't a much bigger man than the sheriff is. He kind of beats me, I mean to say!"

"Aye, and he beats me, too," said I. "But help he's gotta have, or you'll never forget this day, Chip. I can't force you to it, because I've given you my word before I came in."

"You don't have to force me," says Chip. "I'm only thinking. That's all that I'm doing. I'm only thinking. I'm trying to work out the right way."

And he sat quietly again. I could see the size of his problem. If the sheriff got the help that he needed, he would use that help to turn around and chase Chip. And Chip, as he himself admitted, was a pretty tired boy. He was tired when he joined me at my mine, and he hadn't had a full night's sleep since that time. He was shaking with weariness, and when fatigue gets into the nerves, it rots them.

"Well," said Chip at last, in a dead, solemn voice, "I've got it, now."

"What have you got?" said I.

"He's got to have back what he had when he started," said Chip. "Because he's played the game straight, and so I'm gunna play it straight with him. I'm not gunna have no cards up my sleeve when I play it with him, partner."

"That's right, Chip," said I. "What will you do?"

"I'll send him back his two horses, and his pack—and some water. Water!" says Chip, breaking out in a mournful way. "Look what I done to the springs, too! I've gotta go back and try to blast it out deeper than ever, and make the water flow again, and build the rocks up around it again, to keep the water cool. Oh, what a lot I've got on my mind, Joe!"

"I'll help," said I.

"Good old Joe," said Chip, and puts his hand on my hand. It was like a woman's gesture.

"You go," says Chip, "and take the stuff to the sheriff. Just ask him if he'll give me an hour's start, for the sport of the thing. And I'll tie myself into the saddle, and try to last it out!"

Chapter Ten

I found the sheriff, spread-eagled on the sand, absolutely senseless. That final effort he had made to get away from the sight of us had been too much for him. But the mere touch of the wet lips of the canteen upon his mouth was enough to rouse him again. There was a world of vitality in that man. It surged up now. I stood by and heard him gasping, and the sound of the water gurgling down his throat.

Then he got to his feet, swaying a little, pressing his hands against his temples, and I suppose that the temples were bursting.

"Where is he?" he growled.

"Look here, Tug," said I, "that kid has played fair with you. He's sent you this water. He's giving you your chance. You're not going after him now, are you?"

"I'd pretty near rather cut off a leg," said Tug. "But I've got my duty before me, and I'm going to do it. I've taken my oath; I'm going to stick to it. I've swore on a Bible, son, that I'd keep the laws in force."

I saw that he was as fixed as iron.

"He didn't beg," said I. "He only asked for an hour's start. You'll give him that, Tug. You're not the man to refuse him that!"

"I'll see him danged," said the sheriff, "before I'll give him an hour's start."

"You'll be danged," said I, feeling pretty hot, as he swung into the saddle on one of his horses, which I had brought up to him from Chip's captured string. "You'll be danged, Tug, when people find out how you've handled this. You've got water, and you've got a horse and saddle from the kid, and still you're going after him!"

I was about ready to fight, though I'm not much of a fighting man, but the sheriff tamed me down with his answer.

He said: "It ain't me that's after poor little Chip. It's

the law. I'm only one finger in the grip of the law, Joe. But I've got to go where she sends me, and close where she tells me to close. I've got no kindness, no friendship, and nothing to give a partner until the law gets me. It don't let me now, and Heaven help my unhappy soul!"

It was a good deal of a speech, coming from a fellow like Tug Murphy, who did most of his thinking by fits and starts, and dished up his ideas in little portions. I had no answer to it, and as the sheriff rode off, I got onto the other mustang which belonged to him and followed.

Out there in front of us, a small, moving finger of shadow, we could see where Chip was riding. Well behind him was the burro.

We passed that burro at the trot. It only shook its long ears at us as though to say that it comprehended what we were up to and was only glad to have man go on his way.

Well, I was sorry to see that burro drift behind me. He was the small ship that had brought my fortune out there into the desert. I had sighted my course for a good many days between his ears. Somehow, he seemed to me just then like my tangible road to ordinary, law-abiding humanity.

I fairly hated Dug Waters. I had very little affection for Chip, even. I only heartily wished that I had been allowed to stay on at my daily grind, chewing out the hard quartzite and taking its gold away in morsels. I never would get very rich at that work. But I'd get on from day to day, with the taste of the calm, lonely life deepening all the while in my mind. For the best company a fellow can have is the stuff that comes up in his own mind during long silences.

Now I saw the burro soaked up by the night that followed us, and far away before me I could now see the outline of the boy swaying up and down a little among the horizon stars—so I knew that he had his mustang at a canter.

"He'll beat me tonight," said the sheriff. "But I'll get him tomorrow. I just wanta keep fairly close."

He spoke with great surety, and he was not a man to be overconfident at that.

He certainly did not catch the boy that night. My brain was staggering with exhaustion. My thoughts would not run in a smooth flow. But the sheriff, like a bulldog, hung on.

And, in front of us, the boy faded out of view. He was too light in the saddle for us to catch him. And that mustang kept on at a steady, good rate.

I was mightily relieved when the outline of the kid melted away from our eyes, wavered back into view, and then was lost again. But the sheriff did not seem disturbed.

"I know where he's going," said he. "I'll catch him tomorrow."

I wondered that he could be so sure of himself, but he held to a steady course, pointing a little west of north all the while. I sighted this course on a star and saw that he kept to it. But after a time I let my head sag. I grabbed the pommel of the saddle with both hands, and so I sat the saddle, more than half asleep, surging to this side, and to that, as the sleep over-mastered me for a moment.

And the mustang followed along behind the sheriff, head down, almost as tired as its rider. Now and then my head cleared a little, and my eyes, and then I looked ahead and saw that the sheriff was pushing along with his head high and his shoulders squared. It made me sick at heart to think of the will power that man was using—and on a job which he hated!

It was the strangest ride I ever had taken. It was the strangest ride that I ever will make!

In the dawn, we saw thunderheads around the mountains before us.

"The kid's in my hand," said the sheriff. He said it without enthusiasm.

And then we climbed through a dizzy pass and dropped into a narrow valley; and at last we saw the boy.

He was going down the slope before us, very slowly. He was riding the mule now, and the mustang followed, and the body of the youngster was all slewed around to one side, so that I guessed he was sleeping in the saddle, held by the rope with which he had tied himself in place.

Now, if you had seen the trail that he was riding, you would have caught your breath. A mule has extra brains in its feet. But even that mule was navigating the trail slowly, step by step. And now and again it stumbled, and rocks rolled before it and went bounding and beating down the sheer fall of the mountainside. But still the boy did not move. He was like a limp, dead thing.

The sheriff set his teeth, and pushed ahead.

He dismounted, and leading the mustang, he went on foot, because that way of going was both safer and faster, for the moment. I never saw a man look worse than the sheriff did this morning. The black about his eyes seemed to be painted on the skin. The skin itself was wrinkled deep with chisel strokes about the corners of the eyes. And the muscles about the base of his jaw were always bulging. He reminded me of a violin, tuned too high, tuned so high that the strings are about to break.

I dismounted behind and went on down that horrible trail and we gained rather fast on Chip.

I began to think of shouting a warning to him, but there was no need of that, for in another moment one of the rocks we dislodged went leaping like a jack rabbit down the trail. It was a good fifty-pounder, and it went like a cannon ball, after a moment. It jumped to this side, and it jumped to that, and finally it went by the mule, and missed it by inches.

The *whir* of it wakened the boy. Up in the saddle sat Chip, and he swayed violently from side to side. Then he looked back and saw the sheriff coming.

It seemed that he could not make the thing out. I suppose he had been traveling so steadily all the night that he could not imagine we were anything less than miles behind him. I saw him rub his eyes and stare again.

Then he went out of the mule's saddle and whipped onto the back of the mustang. He moved like a young cat.

He pulled out a rifle from the saddle holster and turned and scanned us again, with the air of a man about to shoot. But shooting was not really in his mind. He shoved the rifle back again, and then he gave us an exhibition of horsemanship that to this day makes my heart stand still.

For he pushed that mustang into a trot, and once that was accomplished, gravity did the rest. The little horse could not stop. It began to careen and stagger, and slide, from side to side. Sometimes it swiveled halfway around. It was fighting for its life. And Chip's life was in the saddle.

I stood still and watched, my eyes aching with the nerve strain, and there was a sort of disbelief in me, as though this thing could not be.

And there was something about the dazzling brightness of that morning, and the sheen of the rocks, and the voice of the river in the bottom of the valley, that made my senses reel. It was a dreamlike moment, with all of its horror and its vividness.

I say that the river was sounding in the bottom of the valley. It was running white and brown—not the brown of mud, but the brown of the multitude of rocks which were taken bounding along by the current. It was one of those rivers which flow perhaps two months in two years. Sometimes a year would go by without a favorable rain to more than moisten its bed. And then a torrent poured, and the little river became a giant, and a mad giant, at that, and ran all foam and thunder, and shouting, and leaping, and tearing its hair, so to speak.

That was the way it ran this morning. Not very far away, the current would widen out on the desert, and those swift waters would run slowly and more slowly, and finally they would stumble out in a frothing, muddy tide, and one would hear the sands drinking, and so all that dashing water would sink away into the desert and be lost.

I knew that that was what happened to the stream; but looking at it now, I found it hard to think of that final picture, but all my eye was crowded by the actual strength of the little river and the uproar it made, like an army fighting on the ground, and an answering army bellowing and threatening in the upper air.

Half hypnotically that confusion of noises worked on me; that was the greater part in the dreamlike quality of the morning. But there before me, scurrying down the trail, went poor little Chip, and the sheriff was moving more slowly behind him.

I heard the sheriff cursing furiously, and I knew that it was in admiration of the boy's courage. Just then, as he was prepared to make every possible effort to catch Chip, I knew that the sheriff admired the boy more than he admired any other thing in the world.

But that was the bulldog beauty of the sheriff's character. Now young Chip got to the bottom of the slope, and I saw him hesitate, looking first to one side and then to the other.

At the same moment, I could see his dilemma.

Chapter Eleven

I could see, also, why the sheriff had been so sure of the capture of Chip, even long hours before. He had guessed what trail the boy would take, and he had known what the trap was at the farther end of the line.

There was no getting upstream. A cliff came down there in a plumb line to the rim of the water. And the way downstream was blocked by vast masses of rubble which had pitched down the mountainside in an avalanche. Half the breast of the height had been torn away to furnish this thundering confusion, and the boulders lay there as big as houses and piled on one another like stacks of chipped dice. I shall never forget the sheen of the raw edges of them, picked out with glints and wire-streaks of metal ores, heré and there.

So there, between the two arms of the mountain, poor Chip was riding down to that singing and yelling river.

Now that we got lower in the valley, nearer to the face of the water, more and more there seemed to be one stream raging across the earth, and another roaring though the sky above us, the echoes flung down so loudly from the rim rock. And I had a horrible sense of something great about to happen, something that would overwhelm ordinary human nerves.

The thing seemed impossible, too. Just as when you've hunted the same grizzly for a fortnight, studying the sign, measuring the prints, learning the wits of the old campaigner—so after a thousand trail problems solved and as many thousand disappointments, at last you see the rascal before you, unaware of you, and in easy shooting distance, and the thing appears impossible, and you say that it must be another bear—well, in just that manner I looked down there toward little Chip and could not believe that the sheriff was drawing up on him and driving him into a corner.

I had seen that youngster too often at his tricks. He had

baffled grown men too many times. But there he was, against the wall, as it were.

And all at once he looked pretty small, I can tell you, what with the cliff on one side and the great building blocks of the avalanche on the other. Behind him was the sheriff's rifle—and the mountain trail. And in front of him was the mighty roar and the foam of the creek.

In a sense, of course, that was the smallest of his barriers, but it was a living one. It was beating and smashing to pieces boulders the size of a man almost. And what would it do to a horse and rider?

In the middle of that arena, I saw Chip, like a wild animal, turn to this side and to that; and then he looked back toward the sheriff, who was coming on fast.

He threw off the lead rope that tied the mule to the bronco, and when he did that I knew that Chip was about to attempt something. Only—what could it be? I knew that he was as cool as steel, but when he was surrounded by impossibilities, what out was there for him, in spite of his cleverness and his steady nerves, and all that?

He ran the bronco toward the ruins of the avalanche first of all, but as he came under it, I saw him look up and measure the height and mass of it and shake his head.

There was no scaling that wall in a hurry!

He swung back toward the creek itself, and stopped on the verge of it; yes, with the water curling around the forelegs of the mustang. I couldn't help admiring the control he had over that bronco. It might be a mean, kicking, biting wild cat of a horse, but it had courage. Otherwise no rider could have forced it within ten feet of the verge of that creek.

But Chip was staring constantly out across the water, seeing something, as it were, on the other shore. Aye, what he saw there was freedom, or a ghost of a chance of freedom, I suppose. But how could he get across?

Just then a chunk of the bank a little above Chip went down with a roar and dissolved in the thunder of the water, and turned the stream in front of him to a coffee-colored froth. The spume of it leaped as high as a man's head, and higher.

But still the kid studied the face of the creek like the face of a man when one waits for an answer.

Well, that fall of the bank had changed things a little. For it had tumbled into the currents some boulders so huge that even that ripping water could not budge them easily. I saw one of them tremble, roll slowly over, and then lie still again, shuddering, and seeming to grow light-footed, but still not swaying with the water again.

Suddenly Chip gave the mustang the whip. The bronco shuddered and crouched.

The sheriff, before me, threw up one hand and knocked it against his forehead.

He turned his face toward me a moment, and I've never seen greater horror, but what he shouted I could not hear. There was no talking or hearing down there in the maelstrom.

Besides, I didn't care what the sheriff might say. I only cared what Chip might do.

I've heard punchers tell of crowding wild horses too closely, and how they'll jump cliffs rather than be taken. And Chip seemed like that—ready to die, but not to give up.

I screeched at him, I hardly know what. Something about not being a fool, I suppose. But I saw that whip flash twice again, and then the horse jumped.

I blinked, as a man will when a fist flashes under his eyes, driving home on his chin. When I looked again, there was the mustang, perched like a goat, on the big boulder which had just fallen from the bank.

It was an amazing thing to see Chip there, crouched in the saddle like a jockey, and holding the reins hard with one hand while with the other he held the business end of a lariat.

They were only poised for a second on that rock. The wavering of the thing made it a miracle that they could have kept their balance so long as this.

Then the bronco jumped again to a smaller stone. And by thunder, once more he landed and slipped, but did not fall off! Suddenly I told myself that they were going to get across. It was only a thin strip of a creek, but it was as dangerous as a cannon's mouth.

The sheriff and I were both down to the foot of the trail by this time, but we did not ride on toward the creek's edge. We did not even mount. We just stood still, frozen in place, and gaped, and waited for Fate to decide this thing one way or another.

The mustang jumped the third time. He had his head down. He seemed to be trying to use his chin as a fifth hoof when he landed. But the stone that they aimed for this time was almost lost in the spray and the boiling of the creek, and though the bronco hit the boulder fair and true, he went off it with a roll; and he and Chip disappeared.

No, not all of them.

For as the horse jumped, I saw the rope shoot out straight from the hand of Chip, and it landed the noose snugly about a head of rock on the farther bank.

There were horse and rider under water, and the lariat drawn tight like a dark ray pointing.

They came up. I saw the game mustang swimming hard, head upstream, and Chip striking out beside him.

Something hit the bronco—some stone flung by the current.

He went down.

But up he came again, and now, as the lariat held and the force of the current beat on them, they were forced rapidly in toward the other shore, they reached the shallows, and presently the bronco was scrambling up the farther side.

When he got to the top, with the kid beside him, they leaned together. I saw red running on the body of the horse. I saw red running on the face of Chip, and it was a sight that sickened me.

He did not look back at us. He merely tried to mount, but his legs failed under him. He had to lead the pony to a rock and from that he managed to half slide and half fall into the saddle.

The mustang, head down, badly beaten, started off at a hobbling walk, and I could see Chip tying himself to the stirrup leathers, his hands fumbling. He hardly could have finished the job when he lurched forward along the neck of the horse and lay there like a sack.

The sheriff gripped my arm, and his finger tips sank to the bone. I understood. I couldn't look at Tug, for my part. For what would happen when that exhausted mustang fell with the kid on his back? What would happen to little Chip then?

In the meantime, we stood there with the danger of the creek at our feet, and well we knew that neither the one nor the other of us had the courage to try what Chip had succeeded in accomplishing.

Chapter Twelve

The sheriff was ashamed, but I was not. The crossing of that boiling creek was the most foolhardy thing I'd ever seen attempted. But still the sheriff seemed to feel that his duty to the law demanded that he make the attempt.

That would have been suicide. With a grown man's weight in the saddle, no horse that was not a goat outright could have succeeded in jumping from one stone to another and keeping its balance. Even with Chip up, the bronco had only managed to make two jumps.

Still, it was half amusing and half pathetic to see the sheriff promenading on his horse up and down the bank, scowling and shaking his head at the water.

Finally he gave up, and we made camp there in the thunder and the silence of the canyon—the silence of our human voices, I mean to say, which kept us from speaking. But then, speech was not very necessary. Each of us knew pretty well what the other was thinking.

We cooked and ate a meal. We forced ourselves to it, though we were fairly shaking with fatigue. Then we lay down to sleep.

It was late afternoon when we were awakened by the absence of the thunder in the valley. Both of us sat up at almost the same moment and looked a question at the other fellow. Then we went over to the bank of the stream and looked.

Of course, there was nothing very surprising about it. The thunderheads that we saw from the far-off desert had poured their rain on the highlands and sent the rush of the currents down the canyon. That rain was used up. And the bed of the stream was now almost dry. So we had gone to bed in the midst of thunder, and we were waking in the midst of silence.

I cannot tell how to describe what a difference there was in the very look of the valley now that the lion was no longer roaring. Still, the vibration of that uproar was in our memories so vividly that it seemed as though the tumult were only gradually fading away into the distance rather than completely gone. And the valley itself seemed loftier and more grand in all its faces, now that it was not flooded by the noise.

Well, we got the saddles on the mustangs and started forward again. We found it no trick to cross the dry creek bed, of course, and on the farther side the sheriff lined out on the trail of the boy.

It was easily found and read for a little distance, but then it went out. The sheriff struck straight on, in the direction of the boy's first line of flight. He said that Chip was so hurt and exhausted that for once he would not be able to attempt any trickery. But I decided that Chip might be more than half dead, but he would be always more than a fox! I had seen too much of him.

So I parted from Tug Murphy. He might have held me because he had found the saddlebag in my custody, to begin with. But Tug seemed to have forgotten all about that. He was badly broken up by this job that he had before him. He even shook hands with me when I parted from him, and he said:

"Joe, I should have put a bullet into the kid rather than let him get across the creek and safe away. The next time that we meet, maybe you won't want to look at me or be with me, Joe. Because the next time I meet with Chip, I'm gunna get him with a gun, if I can't get him with my hands!"

I couldn't believe my ears. I said:

"Why, Tug, you're talkin' like a madman. Shoot Chip? You don't mean that you'd draw a bead on old Chip, do you?"

His mouth twisted up to one side. "I've said it, and I mean it," he insisted. "You're gonna find that I mean it, old son, and a dog-gone black day for me."

I said: "Man, you need a rest. You need a dog-gone good long rest. That's what you need. You look all battered, Tug. You can't do right or think right, when you're all jammed up like this. You know you can't. You turn in and make a camp for one turn of the clock, and I'll do the cooking for you—"

He shook his head when I had got this far. And I stopped. He merely smiled at me. And then I saw what it was. It was the oath he had taken that was working like a red poison in the veins of poor Tug. By thunder, but I pitied that man! My heart ached for him. I gave his hand a good grip.

"I don't wish you any luck, Tug," I confessed to him.

"Luck?" said Tug huskily. "I only wish to Heaven that you'll find the kid first and that you'll take him away where I'll never be able to see him again!"

And Tug meant it, too!

I have often thought about it, since that day, but I've never been able to understand the man quite. He was a little too simple, too close to the soil for me to have a complete understanding of him. He worked as a dog works, with its eyes and its heart fixed straight ahead on its duty.

Well, we parted that day, and the sheriff went jogging off on one of his horses, and the other mustang he left to me. So I took it and asked myself deep down, where the kid was likely to be and what would have passed through his mind.

His own pain and weakness and his agony for the lack of sleep? No, I couldn't imagine Chip beaten down as far as that. He would always reserve the first place for the affairs of his friend and partner, Waters. And, therefore, he would be concerned only with the safe disposal of that infernal saddlebag with the fortune inside it.

Which way for that purpose?

Why, right up into the nearest nest of the mountains, perhaps!

So that was the way I steered.

That last sleep had done me a great deal of good, but I was tired. I was soaked in weariness clear to the bone, because after you've been through a sleep famine and a water famine together, you need rest the way a horse does after its summer's hauling work. It don't rest up in a day. It stays groggy for two weeks on easy pasture before it begins to pick its head up and see that the old world is not so bad after all.

But I plugged away through the red-hot latter part of

that day, steering for the first tangle of mountaintops that I saw. And on the way there I found mostly rocks that wouldn't take a print, but in one place there were six hoof-prints made by an unshod horse that was going at a walk in the direction I had chosen.

Well, that decided me that I was absolutely right and that Chip must surely have lighted out in the line I had guessed beforehand. So I felt a great deal set up, as you can imagine. This brightened me enough to even get part of a song out of my throat.

I pulled the mustang into a twisting gulley that pointed for the high places, as it seemed to me, and just as I was taking the first elbow turn, a voice sang out behind me:

"Hey, Joe!"

I grabbed my Colt and turned around. My nerves were pretty jumpy that day, I guess. And there I saw Waters riding along behind me. And he threw up his hands and laughed at me.

"Don't shoot!" says he.

I took a good bead on him, which is not a polite thing to do.

"I'd like to blow the lining out of you," says I.

"Sure you would," says he. "You always did want to, sort of. What's the matter with you, old son? I thought you were up the line, somewheres, chewing on some quartzite for a stick of candy."

"Yeah. I been chewing quartzite," said I.

I put up the gun and scowled at him. But he didn't care. He shook hands. There was something a little aloof about Waters. He never seemed to mind very much what other people thought—except for Chip. Chip could get under his skin with a single glance, of course.

"Well," said Waters, "if it hadn't been for quartzite, I'd've been an honest man to this day."

"You?" said I. "You never could be any straighter than the hind leg of a dog."

"What's the matter with you, boy?" says Waters. "You're riding me pretty hard, it seems to me."

"Yeah, I'm riding you hard," said I. "And I'm gunna ride you harder."

"Go on," said he. "I see that you're mysterious."

He laughed a little, softly, and sort of in the high hollow of his throat, so to speak; and then he curled up the ends of his short mustaches and sparkled his blue eyes at me.

Dang him! I about hated Dug Waters, just then.

I said: "Chip is right, it seems."

"Right about what?" said Waters. "Chip is always right, the little rat." And he laughed again.

I hated that affected laugh of his.

"He's right when he says that you're a danged dude," said I.

"Hold on!" said Waters. "Did Chip say that?"

He looked alarmed. I suppose there was a covert insult in the fact that he cared not a rap what I might think of him, but he was pretty badly jarred by the boy's opinion.

"Yeah, that's what he said," I answered.

He looked away from me and then back again, like a man who has received a pretty hard blow.

"He thinks that I'm a dude, does he?" said he.

He said it in a low voice, thinking the idea over.

"You know," I explained cheerfully. "He thinks that you're too fussy about clothes and such things. You know how it is. Curling your whiskers too much, and all that."

Waters blinked.

"Well, I'm kind of surprised," he said. "I didn't think that he'd notice, somehow. You know how it is. I didn't think that he'd pay any attention. You know, old son."

I nodded. "He's got a pair of eyes," I said.

"He's got everything," said Waters.

He meant it, too.

"Well," I said, "he's not blind, anyway."

"I'm on his trail," remarked Waters. "I thought that I might find him farther on, where you were working."

"I'm working now," said I.

"At what?" asked Waters.

"To try to find the kid before the sheriff does," said I.

He flinched. "The sheriff?" said he.

"Yeah. Murphy," said I.

His lips twitched and his eyes narrowed. There was murder in the look of Waters just then. I never saw death and destruction more clearly promised in the face of any man.

"He's been after me long enough," said Waters softly, and almost to himself. "Now I'm going after him."

143

"All right," said I. "You go after him. You catch him. You catch him before he catches the kid."

"He's lining out for Chip, is he?" said Waters.

"Yeah. That's what he's doing," said I.

Waters showed his teeth. "I'm going to kill that blankety-blank——" he promised himself.

I looked him in the eye. "You hurry, then," said I. "Befor he kills the kid."

"Kills the kid?" said Waters.

He was blank enough now. All the sleekness and the smoothness were worn out of his manner.

"That's what I said," I told him.

"Look here," demanded Waters. "What's happened?"

I told him, and I made it strong. I told him how Chip had come, and how the sheriff had tailed him in, and how Chip had nearly been the death of the pair of us, and how he had come up in time to save us, too, and how the sheriff had started on his trail.

I told about the riding of the river, too, and when he heard that, Waters put up a hand as though he wanted to ward off a blow. But the blow went home, nevertheless. His mouth began to work for a moment before he could speak.

"I've been a dog to load the kid down with that sort of a responsibility," says he.

"Yeah," says I. "You've been a dog!"

Chapter Thirteen

Things were drawing to a close. I felt that as I went on with Waters riding beside me. I felt also that evil was working in the air, so to speak, and that this trouble might be one big enough to blast everything—Waters, Chip, the sheriff, and myself.

For, somehow, I sensed an inevitable crash, such as one feels when the thunderheads are piling over the mountains. The same picture had been painted before. I mean to say, the sheriff and Chip and Waters and I had all been involved. That time the air cleared. This time I guessed at the worst.

And this is what happened.

We went through a rocky gap into an upland valley, where there was a dark cloud of pines—not big ones, but good to eyes that were so used to glittering rock and white sand.

Out of the distance, even, we could hear the trickling of water, and the soft, easy song of it; and riding up that valley, we took off our hats, I promise you, to the smell of the clean pines, and breathed it to the bottom of our souls.

It was pretty cold. I had piled my slicker on top of all the rest of my outfit to turn the edge of the wind, and when I saw a twist of smoke above the trees, I suggested to Waters that we go in there and warm our hands, at least.

Waters stared at me.

"Why d'you think that we've been going in this direction for the last mile?" he asked me.

"You saw the thing from away back?"

"Yeah. I saw it. Maybe it's what we want."

"Chip?"

"Or the sheriff," said Waters.

"Come along, man," said I. "You're not hunting for trouble with the sheriff, I know. Let the sheriff go. He's only doing his duty."

"I'll only be doing mine," answered Waters, "if I blow his head off. I'll take a chance with him, anyway."

I argued no more. There's no use arguing with a bull terrier. You may beat him half to death, but in the finish he'll put his teeth as near the other dog's life as he can.

So it was with Waters. His face was gray when he thought of the sheriff, and his nostrils worked. I don't think it was because he laid such a great heap of blame on old Murphy; it was because he was ashamed on account of Chip. When a man is ashamed, of course he's a ton more dangerous than when he's justly angered.

Well, we went on through the woods, and we came at last close up to the smoke, and I was for riding straight in, but Waters slides off his horse, throws me the reins, and goes sneaking ahead on foot.

After a moment I heard a shout, and I went crashing

straight through to find Waters doing his war dance in front—not of the sheriff, but of young Chip.

And Chip was sitting up with his back to a tree, and on his wrists there were handcuffs, and from the handcuffs ran a rope that circled the tree. His blankets were under him, and it looked as though he had been sound asleep when Waters discovered him. I mean, his hair was all tousled and he was yawning and laughing at the same time.

They began abusing each other in a good-natured way.

"You pie-eyed little snake," says Waters, "what made you crawl away off up here? I never gave you any such marching orders as that. What brought you up here?"

"I'll tell you," said Chip. "I just got tired of riding alone, so I came up here and found the sheriff."

"He was pretty glad to see you, I guess," said Waters.

"Yeah, he was glad," said the boy.

"So glad he wanted to be sure you'd be here when he came back?"

"That's right. He put these things on me just to remind me to stay. There ain't hardly any attention that the sheriff don't seem ready to pay to me!"

He laughed a little as he said it. Then he nodded to me.

"Hello, Joe," says he.

"Hello, Chip," says I. "How does it go?"

"You know," says Chip. "It goes along all right. I ain't dead, and neither is the sheriff. So there you are."

"Where's the sheriff now?" asked Waters.

"He's gone off to have a look for some venison," said Chip. "He says that he could eat a whole saddle all by himself."

"I hope he has luck," says Waters, "because he might have some help in the eating of that venison. He might only be the host, in fact."

Chip looked him squarely in the face. "You mean to make trouble with him, do you?" said he.

"Why shouldn't I?" said Waters. "How much trouble has he made for you and me?"

"Leave me out of it," said the boy.

"Yeah? Leave you out, Chip?"

"Yeah. I've got nothing agin' the sheriff," said Chip.

"Come along," said Waters. "He's hunted you like a fox."

"That's what I've been," said Chip. "He had a right."

146

Waters merely blinked.

Chip went on: "You poke a man in the nose, ain't he got a right to poke back?"

"Why, I suppose he has," said Waters.

"You bet he has," said Chip.

"When did I hit the sheriff?" asked Waters, scowling.

"Whenever you broke the law," said Chip.

Waters snapped his fingers.

"You like that Irish stiff pretty well, don't you?" said he.

"What's better blood than the Irish?" says Chip.

"Oh, bah!" says Waters.

Chip growled in his throat.

"You'd rather have your dang English blood, I reckon," says Chip. "You'd rather be one of them sneakin' aristocrats, maybe, or my lord what-not, and of all the lyin', sneakin', worthless—"

"Shut up," says Waters, very hot.

"I won't shut up," says Chip.

"You will," said Waters, "because I'll make you."

"Give me my hands free and it'll take two like you to make me," says the boy.

"I'll free your hands for you," said Waters. "A thrashing is what you need. A good caning, and I'm the man to give it to you!"

"The whole blankety-blank red-blooming island of England couldn't thrash an Irishman!" screamed Chip.

"Any one Englishman is as good as three Irishmen," says Waters.

I thought the boy would twist himself into a knot.

"You lie!" says he. "You lie, and you lie ten times, and if I had my hands free I'd show you just how bad you lie!"

Waters was just as hot.

"Policemen and boodle grabbers and crooks is all that Ireland turns out," says Waters.

"Real crooks is what they turn out," said Chip instantly, "and not poor, dawdlin' excuses like Dug Waters!"

"You little puppy!" says Waters through his teeth.

"The sheriff will be back in a minute," says Chip. "You'd better run for it as fast as you can, because he's Irish, too, and when he catches hold of an English-American like you he'll just start in by bashin' in your face for you, and I wouldn't like to see your skin broke,

147

Waters, because it would give everybody a chance to see the yaller that's in you!"

It was foolish business to try to talk down that boy. When he got worked up to it, his punch in language was worse than the punch of any man.

Waters looked to both sides at once, so to speak, but he couldn't find a proper answer. I came in and tapped his shoulder. "It's no good," said I. "You cannot keep that game chicken still. Don't try, old son. He'll always win out."

"Wait till I free his hands," said Waters. "I'm going to teach him manners. That's all I'm going to do. He's too long out of school. That's the trouble with him."

"I'll show you what I've learned out of school," says the kid.

Waters leaned over, and with a little picklock, he barely touched those handcuffs, and they fell away.

"I wouldn't even get up to pay no attention to you, Waters," says the kid.

"I'll warm you up enough to move you," says Waters. And he catches up a flexible switch from the ground.

I stepped in front of him and caught his hand. "Dug," said I, "you're making a wrong play. You can't touch the kid. You know that you can't."

"Back up," says Waters. "You want a hand in this, do you? If you do, fill your hand before you start."

I was badly scared. Of course, all he wanted was a chance to explode, and he would a lot rather have me than a mere kid to work on.

"Dug," I protested, "I'm begging you to take one turn up and down the clearing here. After that I'll do whatever you say. I'll fill my hand, if I have to."

"You'll fill it now!" says Waters.

He was white. The evil spirit was in him. It was no sight for any one to see, not even for a grown man. And it put me pretty far back. It lowered my temperature a good deal to face him, I can tell you.

But after all, there's a point when even a rat is cornered. And I was cornered then. Somehow, I think that I would have knuckled under, except that another person was watching, and of all people that witness had to be Chip, who himself had no fear!

At any rate, I reached for the handle of my gun and found and gripped it.

"Start your play," said Waters, or rather, the evil spirit that was in Waters then.

But just at that, with a split part of a second to go, Chip pushed in between us.

"Leave off this!" says he.

"Get out of my way!" says Waters, and with a backhand cuff, he knocks the boy sprawling.

Then he saw, in a flash, and I saw, too.

There wasn't enough force in that blow to have floored the real Chip, made of rawhide and whalebone as he was. But the boy had gone down, and staring in wonder at him as he lay on his back, I saw a red-stained bandage around his right leg, above the knee; and Waters saw it, too, and groaned as though a bullet had torn through his own flesh.

Chapter Fourteen

In an instant Waters was down on his knees. Chip, clawing and fighting to get to his feet, whacked his small fist into Waters's face to knock him back.

He might as well have hammered on cast iron, on white iron.

"Hit me again, Chip," said Waters. "I want you to. Slam me good, Chip. It's coming to me. I hit you. I did it! Heavens, what a cur I am!"

Chip sat back against the tree. He put his hand to his face and wiped away a drop of red that was rolling down from his mouth toward his chin. I don't think that Waters had hit him very hard, but just enough to break the thin mucous membrane of the lip.

"Suppose you fellows leave me be for a minute," says he.

"No, no, Chip," says Waters. "I want to tell you that—"

I grabbed him by the shoulder—for I had seen—and whirled him away. He was pretty angry at being manhandled in this manner, but he endured it. I got him through the trees until we were just out of sight of the little fire by which the boy was lying.

"What the dickens do you mean by this?" asks Waters, turning on me again.

"You chump," said I, "Chip was beginning to cry! Didn't you see that? The tears were coming into his eyes."

Waters put his hand against a tree and braced himself, closed his eyes and groaned.

I wanted to make him suffer a little, but hardly as much as this.

"He'll pull out of it all right," said I.

Waters shook his head. "He'll never forgive me," said he. "He must have known that you saw it. He'd forgive me the other things, and even the blow. But never for shaming him. Never for that! There's too much proud Irish in him for that!"

Then he added: "Was there blood on his face?"

"Aye," said I.

Waters groaned again. He began to walk up and down along a short course.

"I've drawn blood from him," he said, "and you know what he's done for me?"

"I know something," said I.

"He's shed his own blood for me! He's dared everything. Just to please a whim of mine, he's done it."

"He's a grand kid," said I. "There's nobody like him."

Waters cursed softly and steadily for a moment.

"I've been nothing but a curse and a drain to him," he declared. "But I wanted to make up, one day, when I had my pile. Then I would have put him in clover. You know. I would have fixed him in the greatest style in the world. I still will. Only—I know that he won't take it. He'll never look at me again until he's old enough to go gunning for me!"

I nodded. That seemed pretty clear. Everything about that lad was the clear strain, and he was not the likely one to forgive or forget insults.

Then I remembered. I said: "He loves you, old son."

"Aye, and that's why I've treated him like this!"

"Well," I told him, "you know, Dug, that every one worth knowing understands how to forgive a friend. Chip is worth knowing."

He whirled about on me. "You saw that bandage?"

"Yes," I said, "I saw that bandage."

"That cur of a sheriff drilled the kid before he got him," said Waters.

"It looks that way," said I.

"Then I'm going to get Murphy," declared Waters. "And I'm going to get him good."

He continued walking up and down. He controlled his voice, and it came out steadily.

"I had my wad. A quarter of a million—that's enough for a start. It's enough for me to begin on, and try to make my way. If I can't do it with that, I'm no good at all. You know, Joe, that I've been no good all my life. I've taken the easiest way. You know why I want to take the hard way and be straight?"

"Because of Chip," said I, getting a flash.

He was amazed at me. "How did you guess that?" said he.

"Well," said I, "because Chip is straight himself, and because he means more to you than any one else does."

He nodded slowly, like a man thinking a thing over from the start.

"That's right," said he. "It's Chip. He's so dang straight. You know what used to happen?"

"What?" said I.

"Well, after I'd made a haul—sometimes Chip had helped me more than a little—I used to try to split the proceeds with him. I used to try to give him his whack. But he never would take it. He used to say: 'I work for the money that I get.' Mind you, he never used to tell me that I was a crook or anything like that."

"He loves you, old son," I repeated.

"I'm going to give him the best break in the world," said he.

"Of course you will," said I.

"Murphy drilled him!" said he.

"Murphy had his duty to do," said I.

"Duty? To shoot a kid?" said Waters, boiling.

"Yes. Duty means a lot to Murphy."

"Duty's going to bring him to his grave," said Waters.

"Well, he knows that," I answered.

He stared at me. "Knows what?"

"He knows that this job'll be the finish of him. It's no pleasure to him to go gunning after kids."

151

"You're a friend of his, it seems," says Waters, cold and still.

"Yes," I answered. "I'm a friend of his. He's one of the best."

"I'm going to kill that friend of yours," says he.

"You'll hang for it, then," says I.

"It's not the first man that's gone down when I pulled the trigger," says he, sneering.

"It's the first honest man," says I.

"What?" shouted Waters.

"Why, you poor loon," says I, "you've never taken a fall out of an honest man. Not with slugs. Crooks and thugs, on one side of the law or the other, you've put them down. But you haven't put down the straight shooters. You know it. You've used your guns where the using was pretty near a virtue. Am I wrong?"

He stared again. "You're trying to make me out nearly virtuous, aren't you?" said he.

"Aw, Dug," I answered, "you've never been a bad sort. You've taken the easiest way, almost always. But that's the end. Your heart's been straight."

He gaped. "All right," said he, "if that's the way you think about it." But he was badly dented by what I had said, and he showed it. "D'you think that I can go back to the kid now?" asked he.

"Of course you can," said I.

"Well, I'm going back to ask his pardon, on my knees!" said Waters.

"I'll walk the other way," said I. "I'll give you fifteen minutes to do what's right."

So I took a walk through the pines, and I waited until I thought that the fifteen minutes were about up, and then I added another quarter of an hour for luck. And the pines were as still as a funeral, and even the squirrels scampered along the branches and had lost their voices, or so it seemed. And as I walked there, I got to thinking about Waters, and Chip, and the sheriff, and wondering how the thing would turn out, but all that I could see was murder, in the end. Because Waters would never forgive the sheriff for the bullet that he, a grown man, had put through Chip's leg.

Finally, when the time was twice up, I strolled back, and got the smell of the fire through the trees, and then I followed on and came to the place where Chip was lying. He was stretched out on his back, and Waters was beside him, and Waters was talking, and this was what I heard:

"You know, Chip, that dog-gone dog knew all about me. When I came down in the morning he gave a sniff to my boots, and he knew by the sniff of them whether I was going out hunting or not. If I were not going, he went and curled up in a corner and went to sleep again. But if I was going, then he'd just follow me at the heels all around the house, and crawl under my chair at breakfast."

"Jiminy," says Chip. "That's the kind of a dog to have!"

And he laughed a little. Then he said again: "Wouldn't I give my socks for a dog like that!"

"I'm going to tell you something," says Waters. "That dog is going to be yours. That very same dog."

"Go on!" says the kid.

"I mean it. He's yours."

"I wouldn't take your dog," said Chip with a quaver in his voice.

"Everything that's mine is yours," said Waters. "You know that. We've agreed that."

"Jiminy!" says the boy.

"And then," says Waters, "you're going to pick out a school that you like and you're going to go to it!"

"On what?" says Chip. "It costs money to go to school."

"Aw, I'll find the money. Don't you worry about that," says Waters, and he laughs a little.

"Have you got it?" says Chip.

"Yes, I have it now," says Waters.

"Then it's crooked money!" says the other.

Waters jumped. "Hold on, Chip!" says he.

"I mean it," answers the kid. "It's crooked money, and crooked money is not good enough to buy me a sardine sandwich. Let alone sending me through school."

I listened, and my heart nearly stopped. I could guess that this was worse than a bullet through the heart of Waters. But he held on.

"Suppose I make honest money?" says he.

"Save it, then," says Chip, "and make yourself into an honest man. I'm mighty tired of having a crook for my best friend."

There was a little silence after this. And I began to back

153

softly away. It was a scene I could understand where there was no real place for me, so I just backed out of it.

And the last that I could see of them was Waters sitting rather humped over, thinking. And both of them not saying a word.

Chapter Fifteen

Well, the next thing that I said to myself was: "What about the sheriff? And what would happen to him when Waters got on the trail?"

So I just dropped down the valley a little in the direction in which the kid had waved when he said that the sheriff was off looking for venison.

Perhaps there was very little that I could do. On the other hand, if I saw old Tug Murphy, it might be that I could turn him. I doubted, but I was willing to try. It was worth any effort to stop the meeting if it could be managed.

So I went on through the woods, feeling smaller and all the while more ready to turn back on my traces. And by and by, what do I see but the sheriff himself!

Yes, there he comes riding out of the woods, and a nice picture he makes, with the deer meat packed around his saddle, and his rifle balanced across the pommel, and the wind furling up the brim of his hat above his eyes.

I had an idea. I backed away behind a rock, and from that shelter I drew a good bead on the sheriff with my revolver as he went by, and when he was right opposite to me, I sang out: "Hands up!" And I added a couple of good long curses to make the thing sound more real to my own ears.

Tug Murphy's horse stopped of its own accord—which was enough to make me laugh later on—not just then.

Then Tug sang out: "Who's there?"

I yelled: "Never mind who. One that'll drill you clean if you don't stick up those mitts of yours."

He was actually beginning to raise his hands when suddenly he said:

"Why, it's old Joe!" And he laughed, and simply turned his horse around toward me, still laughing as it wheeled.

"Put them up!" I roared at him again. "Put them up or I'll let the light through you!"

He sat in his saddle with one hand on his rifle and one hand on his hip, and he laughed at me, and the bull-like bellowing of his laughter still, in a sense, is ringing in my ears.

I actually tried to pull that trigger, but I couldn't; and he knew I couldn't; and I knew that he knew I couldn't.

"A rotten murderer is what you make, Joe," says Murphy.

"I'd like to plant you one between the eyes," says I.

"Come out from behind that rock, will you?" says the sheriff.

I came out, with my gun still in my hand.

The sheriff just grinned as he looked me over. "You ain't the kind that could shoot an old partner," says he.

I looked soberly into the face of the sheriff. He was quite a new man. He had lost thirty pounds, I think, in his hunt for Chip. His clothes sagged on him as if his body were a mere scarecrow frame.

"Old son," said I, "you come close to trouble when you didn't shove up your hands."

He shook his head. "You ain't that way," says he. "But so you come up here and found me, did you?"

"Yes," said I, "I found you. And I found the kid, too!"

The sheriff's brown face turned yellow.

"I couldn't run my hoss no faster," he said. "And I begged him and hollered to him to pull up. But he wouldn't. And his weight, it was a mighty lot less than mine, and pretty soon his pony begins to gain on me; and so I up and fired. And I meant to fire lower. I aimed just to chip a nick in the calf of his leg for sort of a warning, but just then his pony gives a big jump—"

He paused. He raised a hand to his face, but could not screen the agony that was in it. I was pretty deeply touched with pity.

"It's all right, old son," said I. "I understand."

"You understand, Joe," says he, "because you're my friend. That's the reason that you understand. You understand because you've got a heart in you, and you know what my duty means to me. But other folks ain't going to understand. This here is my last job as sheriff. They'll laugh me right out of office. I'll have to resign. It's the finish of my career. And—maybe I'm glad of it!"

He was *not* glad, though. The pain was still staring at me out of his eyes.

"Aw, go on, man," said I. "Don't you worry. Besides, I've got something else to tell you about. Don't you go blundering back to your camp fire so dead careless and free as you were riding along just now."

"Why not?" says he.

"Because things are not there as they were when you left the place," I told him.

"What's happened?" he asked me.

"Chip's free," said I.

"Free?" he exclaimed.

I wanted to let the news in on him gradually.

"Yes, free."

"Man, man," he shouts at me, "if you've been tampering with the irons that are legally—" He stopped himself. "How did you manage it?" he asked curiously. "Did you smash 'em with a rock?"

"I didn't do the trick myself," said I.

"Not yourself? Was somebody with you?" says the sheriff in a suddenly grave and quiet voice.

"Aye," said I. "Somebody who simply seemed to touch the lock and it flew open."

"You mean it's Waters!" says the sheriff with a snarl in his throat.

I nodded. I said: "Now's the time, old fellow, to play cautious and to back up. You know that Waters is too handy with a gun for you to have a chance with him. You know that."

"It's Waters," says the sheriff, his face turning grayer than ever. "Then I guess this here is the last day that I'll ever see the sun!"

And as he says this, he gives a wild sort of a look around him, and then upward through the green gloom of the trees to where flecks of blue were shining.

I merely laughed at him.

"You're wild, sheriff," says I. "You'd be a fool to take on a fight with the two of 'em armed to the teeth, and expecting you to come back. Nobody ever would ask you to do it—"

"Nobody ever would," says the sheriff, "but the oath that I took to the people. That would make me. Joe, so long for a while!"

And he wheeled his horse about and goes plunging at full speed up the valley through the trees toward the site of the camp.

I followed as fast as I could leg it. I could have spotted an antelope fifty yards and beat it in a mile, that day. And with every jump of me, my heart was crashing and dashing right in my throat.

But I saw the sheriff, riding like a madman, swirl out of view through the trees, and then, a moment later, as I strained and struggled to sprint faster, I heard two voices shouting loudly, and then the rapid clanging of shots. And then there was silence.

Not the same silence as before, but a thing that crawled and reeked in the very air around me.

Then, as I came closer and broke through into the ring of the trees, I saw a thing to make your blood run cold.

I saw the sheriff down, shot clean out of his saddle, as I supposed. And I saw the great Waters down, too. And the sheriff was pulling himself together and starting for Waters, and Waters was already getting to his feet, very white in the face, and with a shine in his eyes.

Chip has hobbled to the place, and as Waters tries to drive forward, with his gun lifting, Chip throws his arms around him and begs him not to shoot.

"Or they'll hang you, Dug!" he screams. "They'll hang you! They'll hang you!"

What a thrill and a screech was in the voice of that boy. It was like the horrible cry of a frightened woman. But deeper than that. And more in it than that. It was Chip himself; the old indomitable Chip, who was crying out like a girl.

"Chuck up your hands and tell me that you're beat," said Waters, "or I'll surely kill you, Murphy—you boy murderer!"

"Guard yourself!" says the sheriff, and brings himself to his feet, with a gun in his hand, too.

"Make your move!" says Waters, trembling like a tiger.

"Make your own move first, and I'll blow your head

157

off," says the sheriff. "I'm gunna take you in. I'm gunna take you in with a rope around your neck—" But he wavered where he stood. I managed to get in between them.

"Stand away, Joe, or I'll go at him through you," shouts Waters.

"He's helpless!" I yipped over my shoulder, a chill shooting faster than a bullet through my spinal column. "He can't move his shooting arm."

"You lie!" says Murphy. "You lie—you've always lied, you yellow—"

But then he reeled outright, and I caught the gun out of his hand. He staggered, and as he sloped toward the ground, I caught him.

There we laid him out. And there we cut away his clothes and saw what had happened.

The bullet from the gun of Waters had gone straight through the body of the sheriff. And in going through his body, it had gone through his right arm, too. How he had managed to keep a grip on his revolver, I can't tell, but he had done the thing.

Waters was over his fighting madness—there was no other word for it—by this time. He was helping with the care of the wounded man. And when he saw the direction of the wound, he said to me slowly:

"What made him stand up there like that? What made him ask for it a second time?"

I looked back into the eye of Waters.

"Don't you know?" said I.

"He was game. He was dead game," said Waters. "I never saw a gamer one than he. But what made him stand up there like that, when he was a dying man?"

"It was the oath that he took to his people," said I, "when he took office. That's what made him stand up. And who are his people? Why, you, and I, and Chip, and everybody on this range! And now he's a dead man, and Heaven forgive the lot of us—because the law never will!"

Chapter Sixteen

No, he didn't die. I know a doctor who saw the scars, afterward, and who said that he *must* have died. And I remember how we fought to save him.

We had three wounded men in the camp, but the wound through Chip's leg was doing well. And the graze of the bullet that had clipped along Waters's head amounted to nothing. So all three of us worked on the sheriff night and day.

And the weather turned colder, and we had to build a lean-to, and the food played out; but we kept on at it until one day we looked down into the ghostly face of the sheriff and saw that his eye, at last, was clear and strong. He said nothing, but we knew that he would live.

And live he did.

That day Chip drags the saddlebag containing the stolen money to Waters, and points to it. There's a great, dark stain covering half of the leather.

"What did that?" says Waters.

"The sheriff. He bled all over it," says Chip, and he stands there, looking first at the bag and then at Waters.

"What do you want me to say?" asks Waters.

But Chip says nothing, and merely fastens his look straight on the eye of Waters.

Waters moistens his lips.

"What's in your mind, Chip?" says he.

"It's in my mind," said Chip huskily, "that there's still a chance for you, Dug. If you'll try to take it!"

Says Waters: "You mean for me to give up this? This is a fortune! This is yours and mine, kid—with a slice for Joe."

"Joe don't want it," says the boy. "And I don't want it. There's blood on it. And there's blood on you, too, so long as you keep it. You're stained with blood already, but not this kind. The other things that you've done, they'll wash off, but not this!"

Waters blanched. He looked from Chip to me. And I nodded gravely back at him.

"What would you do if you were me?" says Waters to the kid.

And what Chip answered stunned me like a club stroke.

"I'd go in with Murphy," said Chip. "When he can ride in, I'd go in with him, and give up the loot, and take your chance with the law, and try to get clean. Because you're stained, and that's the truth! You're worse than a pig! You been wallowin' and takin' it easy in worse than mud. That's what you been doin'!"

That was how the miracle happened which caused so much talk.

It was Chip's idea, and Chip's persuasion that worked it. And the result was that we all went down to town together, and in the dark of the night we all came to the jail.

The sheriff was completely puzzled.

"I dunno what to think," he confided to me. "I've tried to do my duty. But it looks as though my duty's bein' finished for me by other folks. An oath is a terrible powerful thing, Joe. Look how it's working on all these others! Heaven knows what'll come of it. I hope not too much harm to Waters. The rest of us, we're puppies. But he's a growed-up bear!"

I suppose that there was truth in that. I never saw a nobler face than that of Waters, calm and resigned, as he gave himself up.

One hand was behind his back, however, and that hand gripped hard the fingers of Chip.

But this I was the only one to observe.

It was a strange act, and a great act, in its way. And it had a great result, I'm thankful to say. For when the governor heard of the return of that quarter of a million and of Waters's resolution to lead a life with clean hands, he sent down a pardon that freed Dug from jail, and left him with no trouble in the world except worry about Chip and Chip's future.

But, for that matter, there were already half a dozen strong men worrying about the very same thing.

Only Chip was at ease. And he went off on a hunting trip with Tug Murphy, and left his partner, Waters, behind him, to sit down and do the thinking about the future.